MW01135298

Chosen Wolf

CURSE OF THE MOON - BOOK TWO

STACY CLAFLIN

www.stacyclaflin.com

Copyright ©2016 Stacy Claflin. All rights reserved.
©Cover Design: Rebecca Frank
Edited by Staci Troilo

This is a work of fiction. Any resemblance to actual persons living or dead, businesses, events, or locales is purely coincidental or used fictitiously. The author has taken great liberties with locales including the creation of fictional towns.

Reproduction in whole or part of this publication without express written consent is strictly prohibited. Do not upload or distribute anywhere.

Receive book updates from Stacy Claflin: sign up here.
stacyclaflin.com/newsletter

CHAPTER 1

Victoria

THE FULL MOON INCHED HIGHER in the night sky, growing bigger and brighter by the moment. One by one, the members of the pack ran behind the Moonhaven mansion to remove their clothes before they tore to shreds as their bodies turned from men to wolves. Howls sounded in the distance.

Toby squeezed my hand, holding my gaze. "Maybe this will be the month you can finally shift again, Victoria."

Sharp pains ran through my body. My right hip cracked. I bit my tongue, trying not to cry out in pain. My skin felt on fire as fur tried to poke through, but couldn't.

His face tensed, a pained look in his eyes. "Are you shifting?"

I shook my head. There was nothing normal about this, and it was proving to be more difficult and painful than my other months of un-shifts. Each one grew worse than the last.

Toby scooped me up, carried me inside, and helped me onto my bed. "I can't keep my wolf inside any longer. I'm sorry."

"It's okay." I fought to keep my voice steady. Tears threatened.

He brushed hair from my face and kissed my forehead. "Ziamara's upstairs sleeping. She said to wake her if you need anything."

"I'll be fine." I grimaced, the pain nearly choking me.

Toby cried out and the sound of ripping fabric tore through the room. He spun around and dashed out the door. The back of his shirt had ripped, and fur poked through the split material.

I gripped a pillow, squeezing it as hard as I could to distract myself from the pain. It didn't work, and the pillow exploded, filling the air with white feathers.

A loud pop sounded and then a horrific pain shot through my shoulders. I slumped down and screamed, unable to take the pain.

Ziamara ran in, pulling her rainbow-colored hair from her face. "What's wrong?" She ran to the bed and felt my forehead. "You're burning up. I'm going to get you painkillers."

"No." My voice squeaked. "Find sleeping pills."

Her eyes widened. "You want to *sleep*?"

"I can't do this for a full night. My body will return to normal once the moon goes down."

She stared at me. "Would Toby agree to this?"

"Yes!" I didn't know for sure if he would, and didn't care. He wasn't there to give his opinion.

My wrist snapped and hung like a limp noodle.

"Please!" I begged.

"Okay." She ran from the room.

I grabbed onto the side of the bed, clutched it as hard as I could as a fresh wave of pain ran from my head to my toes. My inner wolf howled and clawed, begging to be set free. I tried giving into the shift, but as usual, nothing happened.

"Can you swallow?" Ziamara's voice broke through my thoughts.

My wolf calmed down, and I managed to open my eyes. "Yes."

"Lean back."

I did.

She swept hair from my face and opened my mouth. "I'm going to put this pill in and then help you with the cup of water unless you want to do it yourself."

I shook my head. With one bum hand, I didn't want to do anything to risk the other.

Ziamara slipped the hard pill onto my tongue and then eased a glass of warm water to my mouth. "Drink."

It took three attempts. I nearly choked, but I managed to get the pill down.

She put the glass on my nightstand, sat next to me, and pulled the covers to my chin. "Close your eyes. I'm going to stay right here."

One of my ankles snapped. I cried out but then managed to close my eyes. Ziamara held my good hand and hummed a soothing tune. I focused on the melody until my mind grew fuzzy. Finally, I lost awareness of everything.

The next morning

WHEN I WOKE, TOBY SAT next to me instead of Ziamara.

"How are you, sweetness?" he asked.

I sat up to discover that nothing hurt and everything moved as though it had never been injured. "Good as new." I forced a smile.

He pulled me close. "Ziamara told me how bad it was. We need to find a way to break this curse. If each full moon only gets worse for you, how will you survive? What if it starts to affect your organs?"

I frowned, having no answer. He was right. "What are we going to do?"

Toby kissed the top of my head. "We'll figure something out. I promise. But classes are going to start soon. Do you feel up to going?"

Lying around wouldn't help me, especially if I fell behind in my studies. "I'm fine."

He helped me up. "Why don't you get ready, and I'll have Brick whip us up some breakfast?"

"Thanks." I got ready as fast as I could and scarfed down the feast made by our pack's cook. All the trauma on my body had left me unusually hungry.

Toby held my hand and led me outside. "Are you sure about going to classes today?"

"It's going to be hard pretending everything's normal, but I'm sure it'll be good for me to get back to life as normal." I ran the back of my hand along scruff on his chin. Shivers ran down my back. How had I managed to snag the most gorgeous man alive? I only hoped I would live long enough to enjoy more time with him.

He pressed his mouth on mine, giving me a deep, mind-melting kiss powerful enough to make me forget about everything else. "I'll miss you."

"Me, too."

Toby squeezed my hand and then climbed into his camouflage Hummer. It roared to life.

I got into the Bentley he'd given me and pulled off my platinum chain necklace, slid it through my cherished engagement ring, and put it back on, tucking it under my shirt and wearing it close to my heart. Unfortunately, I couldn't be seen wearing the ring on my finger because I couldn't tell anyone outside of the pack about the engagement.

The electric gate opened and Toby drove out. I followed him, and it closed behind me. I slowed, letting him get ahead so no one would see us exiting the long gravel drive together.

Once on the road, I headed for the Waldensian mansion. It was my temporary home and housed about fifty other college kids. Had it not been for the full moon the previous night, I would have slept there.

It was early enough that hopefully I could get in and out without anyone noticing my late arrival home. Most would either be still sleeping or just getting up.

My roommate slept soundly. I sighed with relief and messed my covers up so she'd think I'd slept there. Otherwise, her mind would run with wild and untrue conclusions, and that was without her knowing I was engaged to the hottest professor on campus.

Humans couldn't know about us—our true nature. Werewolves weren't supposed to exist, at least not outside of books and movies. So we had to lay low and play by their rules. Sometimes it truly sucked.

I grabbed some clothes from my closet and changed. Time was ticking before my first class.

Sasha sat up in her bed and rubbed her eyes. "What time did you get in?"

"I'm not sure. I didn't check the time."

"Girl, you have some night life." She pulled some braids behind her head and wrapped them in a band. "When are you going to get me into the Jag?"

"I'll see what I can do." I had lost access to the most exclusive club in the area, but I didn't feel like getting into that right then. "Since I'm not seeing Carter anymore, I don't even work there now."

"Oh, right. Massive bummer. Well, if you're bored, one of the sororities is throwing a big party tonight. We need to hang out—it's been too long."

"Yeah, totally. I'll try. Massaro threw another big paper at us and a presentation on top of that. You know, because we have nothing else in our lives other than his course."

"Ugh. Remind me to avoid his classes."

"He's the worst. Do what you can." I grabbed my backpack.

Sasha grimaced. "I can't believe you're still carrying that thing. We seriously need to buy you something cute."

I shrugged. "It works."

"That's not the point."

"Maybe this weekend."

Her face lit up. "Shopping trip! Wanna take the ferry to Seattle?"

I thought of being away from Toby for a day trip. My chest constricted. Weekends were the only chance we could spend any real time together. "Maybe."

Sasha pouted. "Oh, come on. It'll be fun. We can bring along some other girls. You really need girl time."

That actually did sound like fun. "Okay, you've talked me

into it. I'll try to get my paper done by Friday."

"It's a date! Invite your friends. No boys, though. I'm serious."

"No boys. See ya tonight."

"Ciao." She waved.

When I got to the school parking lot, I set the alarm and hurried to my first class. Students surrounded the professor, blocking him from my view. I sat in my typical seat close to the front.

Grace, my fifteen-year-old genius friend, came in and sat next to me, twisting her red hair around her finger. "Can you believe last night's assignment? It took me forever."

"I know, right?" I tried to see around the mob of students clamoring for the professor's attention. The girls could never get enough of Toby. It had been a month since his abduction, but they still acted like he just returned.

She glanced at the girls crowding around him. "They never stop sucking up. You'd think they had a chance at dating him."

I snickered. Grace had no idea just how little a chance they actually stood.

"Okay, time to begin class," Toby announced.

The girls groaned and whined but made their way to their seats. Finally, he came into view. He turned and grinned at me, his eyes shining. I thought back to our parting kiss at Moonhaven, and my body warmed.

He pulled his gaze from me and glanced around the room. "Are you ready to hear about the project coming up?"

We all shook our heads. Just what I needed, another project.

Toby grabbed a pen and began writing on the whiteboard.

"You're going to pair up and come up with a hypothesis. Next, you'll poll at least one hundred people—it should be easy to get double that with social media—and explain why you were right or wrong."

Grace grabbed my arm. "I claim you as my partner."

I nodded. Toby continued explaining the parameters of the assignment. It was hard to focus after being able to be as close to him as I wanted at Moonhaven. My mind kept wandering to stolen kisses and the warmth of being in his arms.

Grace nudged me. "Stop daydreaming."

Was I that obvious?

Almost before it had begun, the class was over. Everyone crowded around Toby again, not allowing me to even give him a little wave. At least I'd be able to give him much more than that later.

"Do you have any ideas for our hypothesis?" Grace asked as we headed down the hall.

"No. Let's think about it tonight. He said we'd break off into pairs tomorrow."

"Okay. I don't have any ideas yet."

"Me, neither." We made small talk as I drove us to the other side of campus.

In my geography class, Professor Johnson stood at the front of the room, poring over maps.

I sat in my typical seat, mentally listing off the countries in Europe for our inevitable quiz.

Someone sat next to me, but I was too wrapped up in my list.

"Hey there," came a familiar, feminine voice.

I snapped my attention to the beautiful, quirky blonde.

"What are you doing here, Soleil?"

She put her hands behind her head and grinned. "I just transferred." She mouthed, *Toby insisted.*

"From where? Valhalla U?"

Soleil sat up, shooting me a dirty look. "Not funny," she whispered. "And don't say that out loud. Even humans know that's where valkyries are from."

I rolled my eyes. "Like anyone's going to believe you're—"

"Don't." She narrowed her eyes, blackness covering the blue, and bleeding into the white.

"Okay, okay." Even if I did say she was a valkyrie, no one would believe it any more than they'd believe I was a werewolf engaged to the hottest professor on campus, who also happened to be a werewolf.

The blue returned to Soleil's eyes, and she smiled. "I was able to get into this and psych with you, too."

I arched a brow. "Couldn't get into stats?"

Half of her mouth curved up. "Actually, no. But with Toby there, you're safe." Soleil leaned close. "This class is going to be a snap. I've been to every country countless times, not to mention a few that she"—Soleil flicked a nod toward Professor Johnson—"hasn't even heard of. I guarantee it. Some things get erased from history permanently."

"Close your books and laptops," Professor Johnson said. "Quiz time."

People groaned around us as she passed out the papers with an outline of Europe on them. "You have exactly ten minutes."

Soleil had hers finished before I had written my name and date.

"Showoff," I whispered.

She smirked playfully and sipped some coffee. At least I assumed it was coffee, but after seeing her drink from souls, I wasn't going to ask.

After class, I couldn't find Toby in the cafeteria.

"He's fine," Soleil bit into her sandwich.

I frowned. "He's usually here."

She gave me a knowing look. "You had him all weekend, remember?"

"It wasn't like we had a lot of alone time with the pack around. They were all over him like a bunch of excited puppies."

"You'll have to get used to that, chicky. There's nothing like the love and loyalty of a pack—especially this one. They're dedicated to him because he's good to them, not because he threatens them like a traditional alpha."

"Yeah, you're right. I guess I can't complain. Part of why I fell in love with him this time—before my memories were restored—is because he spent so much time and attention on his pack."

"And he wants you right there with him." She arched her brows.

I sipped my drink. "That's true." I really didn't have much room to complain about anything. I'd been dead and then had my memories stripped from me. Now I was alive and had him back, including all my memories of him. There were still some blanks, though. I couldn't remember anything about why my memories had been wiped.

But more importantly, I needed to figure out how to shift at the full moon before it killed me.

CHAPTER 2

Victoria

WHEN WE GOT TO THE last class of the day, I turned to Soleil. "Watch out for Massaro. He could probably suck out *your* soul."

The valkyrie's eyes narrowed and the blue turned black. "I'd like to see him try."

I snickered. "Oh, he will. It's just a matter of time. I think he secretly wishes he was a val—"

The whites of Soleil's eyes turned completely black. "I told you not to say that."

"You're going to have to stop doing that. What if someone sees you?"

Her eyes returned to normal. "Then don't test me."

Carter came in and sat next to us. The jaguar shifter eyed Soleil. "What are you doing here?"

"Watching out for my new best friend. Now you can shoo." Soleil waved him away.

He shook his head and stared at me. "I discovered some secrets my father has been hiding."

"Did you learn anything useful, pretty boy?" Soleil asked.

"Why don't you drink from my soul and find out?"

Her eyes blackened, but then quickly turned back to blue. "You two don't understand the severity of this. If someone finds out my true nature, I may be forced to drink the essence from everyone in the room."

Carter's eyes widened. "At the same time?"

She nodded. "It's not pretty."

"You can really do that?" Carter appeared impressed.

"I once had to do that with an entire small town." She frowned. "I was sick for a week. But we're not here to discuss that. Have you learned anything that'll help us?"

He leaned closer and made eye contact with me. "Your father and Toby's are furious about him escaping."

"That's hardly news," Soleil said. "You know, since they planned on *killing* him."

His focus remained on me. "It's probably a good thing she's watching over you."

Blood drained from my face. I swallowed, but couldn't reply.

"Anything about her curse?" Soleil asked. "She needs to be able to shift soon. Preferably before the next full moon."

Carter shook his head. "No, but you guys have that witch on it, don't you?"

"Yeah," I said, "but she'd have an easier time fixing me if she knew what she was dealing with."

"I'll see what I can do, but if I start asking too many questions, my father's going to get suspicious. We can't let him figure out that I'm working with the wolves."

My breathing grew shallow. "Are Toby and I in real danger?"

He nodded and leaned closer, speaking even softer. "My

father wants him dead. It doesn't get much worse than that."

Massaro entered the room and slammed his things on the table. "I'm sure you're all ready for the quiz. Put everything except your pencils away."

I groaned.

Soleil leaned over and glared at Carter. "Meet us at Moonhaven later. You need to tell us everything."

"Silence," Massaro boomed.

We made it through the class without any mishaps, and then I drove Soleil to Moonhaven.

Alex, the wolfborn who only turned human during the full moon, trotted over and sat next to me after I closed the car door. I rubbed the top of his head and sighed.

"Where's the jaguar?" Soleil asked.

"He has another class, so it'll probably be an hour."

"Let's get inside and eat. I'm starving."

"You're worse than a wolf before the full moon."

She scowled. "It's either that or I drink the essence from more supernaturals. Want to volunteer?"

"Hardly. Let's grab a snack."

We headed inside, with Alex trailing behind us. He sat on the porch once we opened the front door. Inside, Jet and Dillon, two young werewolves who didn't usually get along, sat in the front room, playing cards.

In the kitchen, Brick, one of the pack bodyguards and every bit as tough as his name indicated, stood at the stove, stirring something in a large pot. It smelled like stew. My mouth watered.

Soleil froze and stood taller, fluffing out her hair. "Is there enough for a hungry valkyrie?"

Brick turned around. His eyes lit up at the sight of her. "You can have as much as you want. And you arrived just in time. I hope you like it."

She winked. "I'm sure it's perfect—and that's not the only perfect thing in the room."

His cheeks flushed, but he flexed and raised his brows.

I sat at the table in Toby's spot and pulled out my laptop to get some homework done.

"Are you hungry, Victoria?" Sal, the other enormous pack bodyguard, asked.

"Yes, thanks." I ignored Soleil's and Brick's flirting while I ate and brainstormed ideas for the statistics project. Sure, I was engaged to the professor, but I didn't want an unfair advantage in class.

Toby's voice broke my concentration. "That jaguar's outside the gate, pacing. Want me to get rid of him?"

I jumped up and threw my arms around him. "No. I need to talk to him. Plus, I think I owe him an apology."

"You go with her," Toby told Soleil. "I need to talk with the guys."

"Sure thing." Soleil threw Brick a smile and headed for the door.

I walked after her, wishing I could just stay with Toby.

Outside, Alex trotted over and followed us to the gate.

"What's with the wolf?" she asked.

"He's a wolfborn."

Her eyes widened. "Really? I thought they were only a myth."

"Nope. He's the one who brought me here after my memory spell."

As we neared the gate, I could see Carter pacing in front of it. He came near and reached for a bar.

"I wouldn't," Soleil said. "That's electric."

Carter yanked his hand away. "Are you going to let me in?"

"No," Soleil said quickly.

"Why did you invite me here?" Carter exclaimed.

"Because you kept talking about supernatural stuff in the class," Soleil said.

He gave me a look, clearly asking if I was going to put up with her.

I sighed. "I have good news and bad news."

He came closer to the gate, stopping an inch from it. "What?"

"First the good news—you were right. I shouldn't have doubted you because of your father's actions. For that, I'm sorry."

"I can't hold it against you. It did look pretty bad. What's the bad news?"

"The true love's kiss spell worked—"

"Good." He smiled. "You got all your memories back, right?"

"Mostly. I thought you knew that."

He shook his head. "We've hardly had the chance to talk since that night. You're always so busy with the pack, and I have to keep up appearances with my father so he doesn't suspect I want to help you."

"Speaking of that, can we trust you?" Soleil narrowed her eyes.

"Yes. I'm on your side. My father needs to pay for what

he's done." His brows came together and fury flashed in his eyes. "I knew he was low, but I had no clue just how screwed up he really was—I can't wait to give him exactly what he deserves."

"You're mad that he abducted Toby?" I asked.

He gave me a double-take. "Wait, you don't know?"

"What?" I asked.

"I thought you got all your memories back." He studied me.

"Everything about *Toby*. He's my true love. But I can't remember anything after I died and before I showed up on campus. That's still a big mystery."

His expression tightened. "My *father* is behind your memory loss."

I stared at him. "What?"

Carter shook his head. "You spent the whole summer in the Jag. Father kept you locked inside the club the entire time. Yurika from the salon was the one to help you adjust to the modern world."

Dizziness swept over me. I tried to ignore it. "What does that mean for you?"

"It means I'll do whatever I can to help you."

"Even though she doesn't love you?" Soleil asked.

"A little tact, please," I said. I took deep breaths, fighting the growing dizziness.

"Yes," Carter said. "I still care about you, Victoria. And besides, my father has it coming."

I paused, doubting that the pack would be willing to let him join us. Then I knew exactly how he could help us. "Are you willing to be a spy?"

A slow smile spread across his face. "My father is going to get what he has coming."

"What have you found out already?" I asked.

"Not much. He knows I have feelings for you, but if I act mad that you chose Toby, he'll believe I want revenge. He'll tell me everything."

Relief washed through me. Maybe we did stand a chance at figuring out how to get me to shift again. "Thank you, Carter. If I could change things, I would. I never meant to hurt you."

"But my father did mean to hurt me." He paused. "I'll be in touch."

Carter turned around and walked down the driveway, out of sight. An engine started.

Soleil turned to me. "You think he's trustworthy?"

I thought back to the way he'd taken care of me when I hadn't been able to turn at the full moon. "Completely."

"Let's hope."

We walked back to the mansion. My steps were unsteady, but Soleil didn't notice. Alex walked next to me, panting.

I rubbed the fur between his ears before going inside. The guys were all gathered around the kitchen table, deep in discussion.

"What's up with the jaguar?" Jet asked.

"Carter's going to find out what his father knows. With any luck, I should be able to shift at the next full moon."

Jet's nostrils flared. "How do we know he won't double cross us?"

"Because I trust him." I narrowed my eyes.

Toby got up and put an arm around my waist. "If Victoria trusts him, then he's safe."

Jet shook his head but didn't say anything. His mouth formed a straight line and his brows came together.

"Look," I said. "Carter's dad kept him in the dark about *everything*. He's furious about that and wants to make him pay. The best part is his dad will never suspect him."

"Except for the fact that Carter has feelings for you." Jet narrowed his eyes. "That gives him plenty of reasons to suspect him."

"His dad uses money against him. He's not afraid to leave Carter high and dry if he disobeys him—he thinks Carter would never go against him. It's the perfect setup."

Jet grumbled. "I still don't trust him."

"He'll earn it."

We stared each other down until Jet finally looked away. "We'll see," he mumbled.

Toby tipped my chin toward him. "And now we have each other—all your memories of us intact. What else do we need?" He brushed his soft, sweet mouth across mine and turned back to everyone. "We've both escaped the jaguars, and now we know their game. Their power was in secrecy, which has been exposed. *Our* strength is in this pack."

"Not to mention a valkyrie and the most powerful witch in the world are on your side," Soleil added. "Oh, and quite a few other supernaturals from the Faeble."

Toby pulled me closer. "There are also other packs around the world I can call on if push comes to shove. We've got this. Let's sit and enjoy the meal."

We took our seats and Brick brought over more food to the table.

My bones ached. I rubbed my arm.

"Are you okay?" Toby asked.

"Everything hurts when I don't change at the full moon. It's lingering longer than the other times."

Concern washed over his face. "I'm calling Gessilyn. She's working on finding a counter-spell, but I want to find out what progress she and the other witches have made."

"What about changing at will?" Dillon asked her. "For all of us."

"Yeah," Jet agreed. "We don't call it a curse for nothing."

I nodded. "And Alex would probably like to be human more."

Jet's forehead wrinkled. "Wait. What?"

"The wolf outside. His name is Alex."

"Are you saying the wolf that adopted us is a wolfborn?" Jet asked, his expression bewildered.

I nodded. "He brought me here after you guys all turned into wolves."

"I'll have Gessilyn look into that, too," Toby said. "If the jaguars can shift when they want, I see no reason wolves can't. Hopefully, it's just a matter of finding the right spell."

White spread around the edges of my vision. I clung to my seat.

His eyes widened. "Victoria, are you okay?"

I opened my mouth, but no words came. My eyes closed on their own and a flood of screams sounded inside my head.

Another memory was returning. I quit fighting to stay awake...

CHAPTER 3

Victoria

STRANGE COLORS LOOMED AHEAD. DARK, ominous shades covered the sky. Screams and cries sounded in the distance.

I gasped as I stumbled across the border from death to life along with a throng of others crossing with me. Those behind shoved me into the ones in front. The crowd grew louder by the moment. I could hardly think. Everyone rushed to get to the land of the living before the borders closed—it had to be a mistake. An opening that freed so many deceased back into the land of the living.

I wove my way through the crowd until I finally broke free. The various trees and some mountains in the distance led me to believe I was in the Northwest, likely near the land I'd grown up in.

My heart thundered in my chest—a feeling I hadn't experienced since my last breath.

Could Toby be nearby? Or Elsie? I had never managed to find my sister on the other side in all my years there. It was especially heartbreaking after having witnessed our father plunging the knife into her stomach after I'd tried to stop him.

I moved farther from the mob of people leaving the other

side and studied the landscape. A small town nestled in a valley to the west, seemingly unaware of the pandemonium just out of reach. I headed over there to find a place to think.

All I knew was that I needed to avoid the crowd in case someone wrangled them back to the other side of death's door. I wasn't going back without a fight. This was my chance to find Toby. Even if he had moved on with his life and had a family, I needed to at least see him one final time.

Not a day had gone by where I hadn't stopped to wonder what he was doing with himself. No one had reported seeing him on the other side, so I was certain he still lived. I was glad he had the chance. No one deserved it more than he did.

I thought of my father and Toby's—two rival alphas who had wanted us dead. I'd have to be careful not to run into them, lest they send me straight back to the other side.

A thick, daunting fog covered the landscape. I darted between homes and finally stopped when I came to a little playground. It seemed like the perfect pit stop. I sat on a swing and swayed back and forth, breathing in the fresh air deeply. It felt so good to have lungs again.

I wasn't sure how much time had passed as I sat there, but the fog lifted and the sun came out. The noise from everyone crossing over had passed and settled into a pleasant quiet. People came out from their homes, leaving in futuristic motorized vehicles. How much time had passed since my death?

Not a single horse and buggy sat in sight. Those had been moving out of style back around the time of my death, but even so, my father insisted on living life following the old ways, so I'd never been allowed in a motorized car.

Eventually, my stomach rumbled. I needed to find something to eat, but I didn't know where to start. Father had always provided the food for the meals Mother cooked. We'd never been allowed any other food, always bringing our lunches to school.

My stomach growled again, this time bringing with it severe discomfort. I needed to find something soon.

I climbed off the swing and wandered through the neighborhood. Scents of breakfast drifted from some of the homes. I dared not knock and ask for some. Father had instilled a strong fear of humans in all of us kids, insisting they would kill us if they ever found out about our true nature. It was why some in our pack attacked them when in the wolf form.

Maybe it was close to the full moon. That could be why I was so hungry. Not that it mattered—I just needed to eat.

I wandered the streets, staying as far from the opening to the other side as I could. This was my second chance at life, and there was no way I was going to risk being thrown back over.

Delicious scents filled the air. I followed them until I reached a street full of businesses, many of them appearing to be places to eat. That was all well and good, but I had no money.

Or did I? I dug into my pockets.

Nope. Nothing.

My stomach rumbled and I felt light-headed. I had to do something. Maybe I could offer to wash dishes. Father would hate that, but he wasn't around to help me out.

A group of giggling girls stepped out of one establishment. That was where I would try to get some food. I went inside and looked around. Several people gave me funny expressions— probably because my style was so different from theirs. My long, earth-toned dress stood out from their bright, tight-fitting outfits.

People sat at small tables, either eating or holding small plastic books with images of meals. I took a seat at an empty table and picked up a booklet. It had pictures of food along with descriptions and huge numbers. Those couldn't be the prices, could they? One meal cost more than a young, healthy horse.

A lady about my mother's age in a short skirt and low cut top strolled over to me. "What do you want, hon?"

I tried not to stare. "Um…"

"You need another minute?" She snapped something in her mouth.

"Do you have a daily special?"

"Nope. Prices are what you see."

I rubbed my temples.

"You want to start out with a bacon and egg bagel? It's our most popular item."

"Okay." I prepared to run when she asked for my money.

She wrote something on a pad of paper. "Gimme a few minutes. There's a batch in the oven." She walked away.

My mouth nearly dropped. We didn't have to pay first? At least I could eat. I'd ask to wash dishes later. My stomach rumbled loudly.

The woman brought over the sandwich and I scarfed it down. Anything I asked for, she delivered. It was wonderful. I might have to do chores for a week, but it would be worth it.

When I was finally full, she placed a skinny white paper

with numbers on it in front of me. "I'll be your cashier. The suggested tip is on there."

I stared at the numbers in disbelief. How had I accrued such a hefty bill?

"Something the matter, hon?"

"Well, um…" I paused. "Do you take other forms of payment?"

Her brows came together. "Cash or card only. No checks."

"I can do chores."

"Huh?"

"Or I can—"

"Are you saying you can't pay?" Her mouth formed a straight line and her nostrils flared.

"Not with money, but I—"

"How dare you?" she shouted. "What kind of a place do you think this is? I have kids to feed! You have *got* to be kidding me."

"I can—"

She grabbed my arm. "Stay right here, thief. I'm calling the cops."

I froze. "The police?"

"What do you expect? At least you'll be able to eat all the free meals you want." She pulled a rectangular device from her pocket and slid her finger around the shiny part.

I didn't know what kind of witchcraft she was using, but I wanted nothing to do with that or the local law officers. I yanked my arm from her grasp and ran from the establishment.

She called me names. Several men ran after me.

At least I had food in my stomach—and I had died in my

best leather shoes. I kicked it into gear and ran as fast as I could. My body seemed to remember all the previous exercise. Glancing back, I noticed I was lengthening the gap between me and my pursuers.

I ducked between a couple buildings and darted down one alleyway and then another.

They shouted, but couldn't keep up.

All the years Father had made us train finally paid off.

I continued running, even after I was sure they'd given up. No one called for me now, but I wouldn't stop until my body made me. My muscles burned, but I didn't care.

The suburban setting turned into open fields. I could hear farm animals not far away.

I paused in the middle of a grassy field, gasping for air. An apple orchard wasn't far away. Maybe I could rest there and have some snacks when my appetite returned.

"Hey, there she is!" came a masculine voice. The familiarity of the voice sent shivers down my back.

I spun around.

My stomach sank.

Father.

He'd found me.

My throat closed up.

He and several of the lead pack mates ran toward me. I had to run to the orchard—it was my only chance of hiding.

I burst into another run. My joints and muscles cried out in protest. My lungs felt like they would explode.

How had they found me?

My scent. I hadn't even thought to try to cover it up. Having just eaten so much, it would have been even stronger. It also wasn't like I had wolfsbane on me, nor had I seen any of the flowers along the way.

Not that I had time to worry about that now. My aching body begged me to stop, but my adrenaline pushed it forward.

They gained on me.

Who knew what my father would do to me? He probably knew I'd been the one who had been seeing someone in the rival pack. In fact, Toby's father probably told him about us and even boasted of killing me.

I reached the orchard. Though there were plenty of apple trees, they were spread far enough apart to be of little help. Hiding would be a challenge—I certainly didn't have the advantage of a forest.

I pushed forward, afraid of what dying a second time would do to me. Would I be sent somewhere worse than the other side? There were rumors of a nasty jail, but I'd never seen any proof it actually existed.

Maybe death was my only freedom from my father.

If I did manage to find Toby, and he wasn't leading his own pack, married with a bunch of pups running around, then we would be on the run if he still held any feelings for me and wanted to be with me.

Would giving in to my father be the best option? This world hadn't ever done much to protect me. Even in the arms of safety—Toby's—I'd managed to lose my life.

As I darted between trees, my mind went back to that fateful night.

I shook my head. I had to focus. If there was any chance of finding Toby or my sister, I needed to stay strong and fight.

They shouted at me. Shots rang out through the air, reminding me of the night of my death.

Somehow I managed to run faster and dart around more trees. I turned around one and crashed into a ladder.

"Hey!" a voice shouted from above.

I rubbed my sore eye and continued running, but I was dizzy. My feet got tangled with each other and I fell to the ground. I pulled myself up.

Hands grabbed my arms. "I got her!" My father glared at me. "Finally, I get *my* chance with you. Both you girls soiled my reputation with the pack that night, and you never paid."

"Dying wasn't enough?"

"My enemy killed you. All that did was add to my humiliation. Do you know how long it took for me to regain my pack's respect?"

I struggled to get free, but just like the night he'd killed Elsie, he overpowered me. His nails dug into my skin.

Toby's father strutted over, sneering at me.

My jaw dropped. I turned to Father. "You're working with him now?"

"A common foe can make enemies allies."

"Who...?" I asked, but realized I already knew. "You're against Toby?"

"He managed to kill us," my father said, "but now that we're free from the other side of death, it's payback time."

Toby's father glared at me. "And you're going to be the bait."

Blood drained from my face. "What do you mean?"

My father hit me across the face. "Stop talking, girl." He turned to Toby's father. "Let's get to the jaguars. It's time for them to hold up their end of the deal."

Another man wrapped a blindfold around my eyes and stuffed a gag in my mouth. I struggled, but my father held me down. They led me for what felt like forever as the sun beat down before finally throwing me in a motorized vehicle. The air was hot and stuffy. I rolled around with each turn. Muffled music played from somewhere.

Finally, we stopped and they brought me out into the fresh air. I gasped, and lightheaded, wove on my feet.

Someone—probably my father again—grabbed onto my arms, squeezing hard enough to bruise. They led me inside a building with icy air. I walked, stumbling, until someone shoved me to the ground.

"Stay there. You'll regret it if you try anything."

I was in no position to try anything, blindfolded and gagged with no clue where I was.

Footsteps sounded as others came into the room.

"That the girl?"

"Yeah." That was my father. "You got your witch?"

"She's on her way."

"What's the plan?" asked my father.

"I'll throw her in the dungeon for a few days. Once she's good and weak, the witch will strip her of her ability to shift. The girl won't know what's up or down."

My throat closed up. Tears filled my eyes.

"Then we'll spend the rest of the summer getting her acquainted to the modern world and all its technologies. She has a large learning curve ahead of her since she's used to life from a different era. Once she's up to speed, we'll erase her memories of her past, including her time here. Then I'll send her right into the arms of that new professor you want to destroy so badly."

"But you'll let *me* kill my son," said Toby's father.

"And I need to witness it," my father said.

I held in a gasp. My entire body shook.

"As long as you two hold to your end of the bargain."

"We will."

"Indeed."

I needed to get away and find Toby.

Something hard hit me on the side of the head. I blacked out before hitting the ground.

CHAPTER 4

Toby

I STARED IN FRUSTRATION AT Gessilyn across the bed. She sat close-eyed, playing with her blonde ponytail while Victoria lay unconscious between us. She'd been this way for over an hour.

"What's going on?" I finally demanded.

She opened her eyes and gave me a sympathetic glance. "I would assume the rest of her memories are returning. She's thrashing around the same way she did when she recovered her memories of you. I'm speaking silent blessings since this has probably been brought on by a spell."

Victoria sat up and screamed.

I wrapped my arms around her. "Did you remember anything?"

"Yes. It's all just like we thought—the jaguars used me to lure you in. They're also working with our fathers. Carter's father is working with our two old packs because they want us both dead. They're *still* angry about us running away together."

Dread washed through me. "Our fathers are the ones who want us dead—some things never change. The only question is how they convinced powerful jaguar shifters to help them."

"Money." She shook in my arms.

"But the jaguars are far richer than they are." I tried to make sense of it.

"It doesn't matter, Toby. Only that our old packs are working together *with* the jaguars against us."

"Did you send them there?" she asked. "To the other side?"

I nodded. "You'd better believe I killed them after what happened to you. It took some time, but they paid."

Gessilyn came over to us and put her hand on Victoria's arm. "Did you remember everything?"

She nodded. "Well, about that. Some other details are still filling in. They were the ones behind my memory loss. I was right to trust Carter. He had no clue about me until we met at the barbecue. His dad was behind it, but he didn't know what was going on beyond his dad wanting him to keep an eye on me."

Gessilyn took a deep breath. "Killian and I will stay here a little while longer, just in case you remember anything else."

"I don't think there's anything left," Victoria said. "If there were holes in my memory, I would know."

"Didn't you say some things are still filling in?" I held her closer.

"Just some of the smaller details. It's a lot to take in, but I remember all the major things now." She sighed in relief.

Anger burned at me. "I'm sure it is. It looks like our fathers have more to pay for."

She turned to me. "What are we going to do?"

I kissed her forehead. "We're going to speak to the pack, but not until you're ready."

"I'm ready now." She jumped out of the bed and stumbled.

"Take it easy." I grabbed onto her sides and steadied her.

"I'm just a little dizzy. It's nothing. It'll wear off in a moment." She backed away from my hold. "Trust me. I've been through this before—when I finally remembered our time together."

"The dizziness might linger for a while, though," Gessilyn said. "That's just the way the spell works."

Victoria arched a brow. "You think this is from the spell you placed on me a month ago?"

Gessilyn nodded. "You had a lot of memories stolen. It takes time."

Worry replaced my anger—for a moment, anyway. "You don't think this will happen again, do you? What if she has other memories to uncover that we have no clue about?"

"It's possible." Gessilyn put a hand on Victoria's arm. "You said you think you can remember everything?"

"I think so."

"What about being dead?" I asked. "You spent more years on the other side than you did here."

"I remember escaping. Let's talk to the pack." Victoria pulled on my arm.

I didn't budge. "But you don't remember your time there?"

She shrugged. "There probably isn't much to remember. I was dead." Victoria studied me. "Do you think anything important happened to me then? Anything that could help us?"

"I'm not sure," I replied. "I'm just saying we shouldn't expect your thrust of memories to be over."

She frowned. "Okay."

We headed downstairs. The rest of the pack was in the

family room, watching a movie.

"Are you okay?" Soleil asked Victoria. She and Ziamara ran over to us.

Victoria leaned against me. "Just a little worn out."

"Time for a pack meeting," I said.

Jet paused the movie and turned to Victoria. "Did you remember something about the jaguars?"

I helped Victoria sit, and I filled them in on everything she'd told me. "Did I miss anything?"

She shook her head. "Both our fathers want him dead for killing them."

"But why the jaguars?" Brick asked. "What's so important about them?"

I leaned back in my seat and ran my fingers through my hair, pulling on it. "It makes sense, if you think about it. Their culture is completely different, and they have access to different types of magic. I've heard that Central America, where they originated, is full of black magic we rarely see here—things like voodoo and regularly bringing people back from the dead. Necromancers are highly sought after."

"Do we have a plan?" Dillon asked.

"I'm working on it." I assured him.

"We'll stay as long as necessary," Gessilyn said. "If it gets to be too much, I'll call on my parents. They're still training me."

"You're the high witch, right?" asked Slick, a Samoan who'd been with me for a number of years.

Gessilyn nodded. "Yes, but I didn't know it for centuries. I didn't even practice magic for long stretches of that time."

Slick gave her a double take. "How could you not know?"

"If you'd never seen a mirror, would you know your nose

is round?" Gessilyn asked.

"Huh?"

"I didn't know because I couldn't see it," Gessilyn explained. "Nobody told me. My mother was killed before she had the chance to teach me much, and I only recently met my father and his family. It wasn't even until my parents were working together with me, now that everyone is back from the dead, that they saw it."

"It's not something passed down from one generation to another?" Ziamara asked.

Gessilyn shook her head. "There's usually one high witch for many centuries, and then a new one arises from a different part of the world. It would definitely be nice if there was some training involved, but at least I have my parents."

"This is all great," I said, "but let's save these questions for later. She and Killian are staying. We need to focus on finding out where my father and Victoria's are hiding while Gessilyn looks for a way for Victoria to be able to shift again. I don't know what the long-term effects could be."

Sal rose from his chair. "What do we need to do, sir?"

It felt good to have my pack on my side, ready for action. "We need to make sure Gessilyn has anything she needs." I turned to her. "What *do* you need?"

"Victoria," Gessilyn said.

Her head snapped to attention.

Gessilyn gave her a reassuring smile. "Don't worry, dear. I just need to see if I can find any additional spells, blessings, or curses placed on you."

"What's that going to involve?" Victoria asked.

"All you need to worry about is sitting still. You might

even be able to get some reading done. I wouldn't recommend doing math problems or typing a paper—I need you still."

"I've got about fifty pages from my psychology book to read."

"Perfect." Gessilyn rose from her chair. "Give me a few minutes to gather what I need, then we'll meet outside."

"Outside?" I exclaimed. It was dark out and a light wind whipped on the sides of the house. Typical fall evening.

She stepped toward the stairs. "The elements are strong this time of year. I want to tap directly into them."

Victoria glanced out the window. "How am I supposed to read?"

"You're a wolf under the moonlight, sweetie. It'll work." Gessilyn rounded the corner and disappeared.

"Do you need anything else?" Ziamara asked. "I don't know what I could do, but I'd be happy to help."

Soleil's eyes widened with excitement. "Oh, I know."

Victoria arched a brow.

"Come with us to Seattle on Saturday. We're going shopping with some of Victoria's roomies."

"You want me to go shopping?"

"It'll be fun," Soleil said. "And besides, the more supernaturals we have surrounding our unshifting wolfy, the better."

Jet nodded. "It's been a while since you've fed from humans, too."

"I drink plenty of bags every day," Ziamara said with a defensive tone.

"We both know it's not the same." Jet put his arm around her and kissed her cheek. "And you'll also have fun with the girls. I know how much you need girl time."

She gave him a playful scowl. "I think you're just trying to get rid of me."

He laughed. "Never. I'll miss you, but I think the day trip will do you some good."

Ziamara turned to Victoria. "I'm in. Just tell me the time and place. What do you think I should wear?"

"What you have is fine," Soleil said. "Anything goes in Seattle—trust me."

Gessilyn returned and looked at Victoria. "Are you ready?"

"Can I go with?" I asked.

She shook her head. "Sorry, Toby. Unfortunately, your presence will only interfere. I assure you, she's in good hands."

"I trust you," I said. "Otherwise, I'd be there with you. Where's Killian? He's welcome down here with us."

"Thanks. I needed some ingredients, so he went back home. He might bring one of my parents or siblings with him. The more witches we have on this, the better."

I swept my lips across Victoria's. "I couldn't agree more."

She pressed herself against me and returned the kiss.

Gessilyn waved her over, and they headed outside after Victoria slid on her coat and grabbed her backpack.

I went into the front room and watched from the window. They headed around to the right. I went into my office, peeked from behind the curtains, and lifted a blind.

They stopped about a hundred feet from the house. Gessilyn laid out a blanket. Victoria sat in the middle with her bag. Gessilyn reached into a pocket and sprinkled something around Victoria. She walked around, speaking and waving her arms around. The moon's glow around Victoria brightened.

After a few minutes, Gessilyn stopped and said something

to Victoria, who in return, dug into her bag and pulled out a textbook. She read while Gessilyn sat next to her, arranging what looked like rose petals.

"What are you doing?" I whispered to myself.

"Apologies, sir," came Brick's voice from behind me.

I jumped and turned to him, my heart thundering. "I didn't even hear you come in."

His eyes widened.

"Do you need something?" I exclaimed.

"Just checking to see how things are going, and if you need anything."

"Only for my pulse to return to normal." I peeked back outside. "It looks like they're fine, and I know Victoria's in good hands."

"Perhaps you should grade your papers."

"You're right. I also need to prepare for tomorrow. I hate winging it."

Brick nodded and then left the room. I glanced outside one more time before settling into my chair with homework that needed correcting. I really needed to hire a teacher's assistant. That had been most helpful when I taught high school math. Then I could focus more on Victoria.

It took twice as long to get through the sheets as usual because I kept checking on them. After what felt like forever, Victoria finally came into my office. I jumped up, knocking over papers, and wrapped my arms around her. "Did you two learn anything new?"

"Only that something is blocking me from shifting."

Gessilyn peeked in. "It's an actual spell, not a blessing or curse. So, that actually helps. I know which direction to aim for."

"How could it be a blessing?" I asked. "There's nothing good that can come from it."

"Not unless the ones applying it see it as a positive thing, and I'm sure they do."

I clenched my jaw. "Jerks."

Victoria gave me a sad smile. Her eyes were bloodshot and she had dark bands under them.

"I should take you back home."

She shook her head. "I drove, remember?"

"Then you should stay in the guest room."

"If I don't start sleeping in my own bed, my roommate is going to start asking questions. We're supposed to fit in, and not raise questions, right?"

"Unfortunately." I kissed the skin next to her ear and pressed kisses to her lips, longing for so much more. I cleared my throat. "Maybe going back to the Waldensian isn't the worst idea."

Soleil popped in. "I'll drive her home. Maybe I'll even crash on the floor." She yawned. "Or would that be weird?"

Victoria shook her head. "Sasha's had friends over. It's fine."

"Perfect." Soleil pulled Victoria away from me and gave me a reassuring glance. "She couldn't be in better hands. I'll drain the life force out of anyone who tries anything."

CHAPTER 5

Victoria

"WHAT ARE WE DOING TONIGHT?" I asked Toby, holding his gaze but wishing I could hold his hand. Holding back my affections at school made me crazy. I couldn't wait for the weekend to finally begin. All week, I'd been focused on studying and projects. I just wanted some down time with him.

"About that…" His eyes widened and he gave me the same look he always did when he had bad news. I'd seen that expression many times in my lifetime. Lifetimes?

"What?" I asked, disappointment already washing through me.

"I have a poker game tonight."

Soleil snorted. "You? I didn't peg you as a gambling man."

He made a face. "Why's that so hard to believe?"

She shrugged. "You just don't strike me as the type."

"I've been teaching math for decades," he said. "If anyone can take on some college professors at a game of poker, it's me."

"Don't tell *them* that," she said. "You look like you just graduated college yourself."

"How long's the game?" I asked. Maybe we could get some time in after.

"Sounds like it goes all night." He caressed my cheek.

My face fell. "Why are you playing?"

He held my gaze, longing in his eyes. "Not because I'd rather be with them than you. It's an exclusive game from the sounds of it, and I'm supposed to be honored by the invitation."

"But what about everything going on with the pack? With me?" I hoped I didn't sound whiny, but I hadn't spent any time with him since the night Gessilyn had done her ritual out in the field next to Moonhaven.

"Awkward," Soleil muttered. "I need to refill my drink." She got up and scurried away.

"Well?" I asked Toby.

He leaned closer. "People are whispering rumors about Moonhaven—the pack. I need to do whatever I can to assuage their concerns. Playing a weekly poker game will make me look normal."

"I see."

He glanced around and then reached for my hand, and gave it a squeeze. "We're already overwhelmed with problems. I don't want to add the humans to our list."

I played with my food, no longer hungry. "Well, I have homework, anyway. I'm going to be busy all day Saturday."

"You are?"

"Remember? I'm going to Seattle with my roommate and some others girls."

"Including yours truly." Soleil returned and sat, sipping her drink.

"And Ziamara," I added.

"Right. I have so much running through my mind, I forgot." Toby turned to Soleil, looking relieved. "I'm glad you're going with her."

"I'm not helpless," I reminded him. "Remember who saved you from the jaguars?"

"I know," he said. "But until we figure out how to get you to shift, we need to be careful."

"Will that help my aches?" I rubbed my neck.

He arched a brow. "You hurt still?"

"Not too bad, but yeah." I rubbed a wrist. "Mostly my joints."

He frowned. "I'll find out if Gessilyn has made any progress. You should only have bone pain around the time of the full moon."

"Tell that to my body."

"Let me know if it gets any worse, okay?"

I nodded.

People got up from their tables and headed for the doors. The next class period was about to start.

"Looks like it's time to get going," Toby said. "Can I see you before you leave tomorrow?"

"We're going pretty early," Soleil said. "Breakfast on the ferry."

He tapped the table. "I could always make a trip over there, too."

Soleil arched a brow. "To hang out with a bunch of freshman girls?"

"Hmm, that wouldn't look good, would it?" He turned to me. "Sunday?"

"When can I move in with the pack?" I asked. "I'm part of it, right?"

"Of course, but we need to keep up appearances. Poker games, living situations, classes—all of it."

"Wouldn't I be safer staying with you guys? Plus, we'd be able to see each other whenever we want."

He shook his head. "Nobody is going to do anything to you with a bunch of humans around. You're safe at school and in your home. And besides, Soleil is following you around like a lost puppy."

"Hey." Soleil glared at him. "Speaking of appearances," Soleil stood. "We'd better go. Massaro's going to fly off the handle if we're two seconds late."

Toby and I held each other's gaze. It was obvious he didn't want to be apart any more than I did.

"Come on," Soleil urged. "You're already on his list."

I couldn't pull myself from my spot.

Toby mouthed, "I love you."

It took every ounce of my self-control not to run around the table and wrap my arms around him. Soleil tugged on my arm. I would take a lecture from Massaro in exchange for just a moment with Toby.

She yanked on me hard enough that I had to adjust my footing so I wouldn't fall. "You're going to make Toby late, too."

"Okay, okay."

We grabbed our trays, dropped them off, and headed for class.

Massaro called for everyone's attention just as we ran through the door.

"Living life on the edge, I see." Carter shook his head.

I slunk into the seat next to him. "You know me."

Massaro glared at us, but didn't slow down his speech about the big presentation coming up—a project that would be worth nearly a quarter of our grade. I pulled out my computer and took notes, trying not to miss a detail—not with as meticulous and demanding as he was, and as Soleil had pointed out, he already had it out for me. She knew because I hadn't stopped complaining about Massaro since the first time he'd picked on me.

After class, Carter followed Soleil and me out of the building. "I'm going to spend the weekend digging into my dad's stuff."

"Any idea what you'll find?" Soleil asked.

He glanced at me. "Hopefully answers. Haven't had any new memories surface?"

I shook my head. "I told you about the last one already. Maybe Yurika knows something."

"She doesn't. Ninety-nine percent of the staff just do what my father says without question. I gotta get to my next class. Call me if you remember anything."

An idea struck me. "What if you work with the other one percent?"

"What do you mean?"

"The workers who don't obey unquestioningly."

He shook his head. "No, they would be the first to tell my father if they suspected anything."

I arched a brow.

"They may give him a hard time, but it's because he allows it. They're his favorite."

My face fell. "Oh."

"We'll think of something. Call me if you find anything." He went the other way.

"Are you ready to party?" Soleil asked. "And by party, I mean shop."

"That's tomorrow," I reminded her.

"I know. It'll be so much fun to go into the city after hanging around here."

"Can't you go anytime you want?" I headed for my car.

"Sure, but wanting to and actually doing are two different things. I've found a place where I feel like I belong. Do you know how rare that happens? I'm happy here. Between your pack and Tap, I feel normal. Speaking of Tap, I'm suddenly in the mood for a strong rainbow drink."

I shook my head. She would have those all day long if she could. "What about Valhalla? You don't belong there?"

She laughed bitterly. "Hardly. It's all business, and valkyries aren't supposed to stop and have fun."

"None at all?"

"In school, we could get detention just for cracking a smile."

My mouth dropped. "Really? Wait. You had to go to school?"

"Death is serious business, and yeah. Years of school. Our headmaster would make Massaro cry. Daily."

I turned to her. "Serious?"

"Serious as a final exam. I'm expected to take out a dictator, remember? It's not child's play."

"Yeah, I guess not." I remote unlocked the Bentley and hopped in. "You sure you won't get in trouble spending time with us?"

"Nah. I have at least a decade before they even give me a second thought. I'll have to have some progress by then." Soleil climbed in the passenger side. "Where are we going?"

"I don't know about you, but I'm hungry, and then I need to go somewhere quiet to study. That means not Moonhaven or the Waldensian. What do you think? The library?" I started the engine and pulled out of the spot.

"Boring. Let's go to the Faeble."

"Right, because a bar full of supernaturals on a Friday night is going to be so quiet."

She rolled her eyes. "We grab some drinks, find out if Tap's heard any good gossip lately, then we hit one of his private rooms. He'll give us any one we want."

"You sure?"

"Of course. He loves me." She grinned.

"Okay. I'll go to the Waldensian first. Make sure everything is good with Sasha. Ziamara's still coming, right?"

"I thought so. That's what you told Toby at lunch."

"Oh, right. But I never double-checked with her. What if she forgot?"

"I'll give her a call while you talk to your roomie."

"Thanks." I pulled into the parking lot at the mansion. "So, you're staying in here?"

"Yes, ma'am." She pulled down the visor and checked her reflection in the mirror.

"I'll hurry. I want to get as much studying done as I can tonight." I grabbed my backpack and hurried inside.

Sasha sat on her bed, texting. She glanced up at me. "You ready for tomorrow?"

I threw my bag on the bed. "Yep. Just gotta get as much studying done as I can tonight."

"You were serious about that?"

"Yeah. What are you planning? To study on the ferry?"

"You're hilarious. I'll have a cram session on Sunday. Pull an all-nighter if I have to. No way am I wasting a perfectly good Friday night on homework. There's a huge party at one of the frat houses. It's all hush-hush, so I don't even know which one yet." She rolled her eyes. "It's supposed to be some ultimate, giant murder mystery party, but with lots of alcohol. Sure you don't want to go?"

I stared at her.

"What?"

"You want a hangover for our shopping trip? And you do realize the ferry is a boat, right? You'll get sick for sure."

"I'm not getting plastered. Geez. Just going to have some fun—and it's way more entertaining to watch everyone else have too much to drink." She batted her lashes. "Sure you don't want to come?"

"As entertaining as that sounds, I'd rather keep my grades up. Get some videos?"

"You know it. So, we're supposed to catch the ten o'clock ferry, right? Ugh, that's so early—especially for a Saturday. Was that your idea?"

"If we want to make it in time for lunch at the Space Needle."

Sasha grabbed a sparkly, turquoise book bag. "I hope it's worth it."

"I hear the view is great."

"It better be amazeballs if I'm going to be up that early."

I laughed. "I'm sure it will be. You still planning on driving?"

"Yeah, the Highlander holds six."

Soleil appeared in the doorway. "What's taking you so long? I'm going to die of boredom out there."

"We're just discussing tomorrow. You're cool with leaving so early?"

"I can sleep when I get old." Soleil winked at me. If she wasn't old now, I didn't know when she would be. She had stories of hanging out at parties hosted by some of the earliest pharaohs.

"Yeah, I guess." Sasha seemed to be considering the logic.

My phone buzzed. I checked the text.

Toby: *Moonhaven. Now.*

Victoria: *What? Why?*

Toby: *DB*

My mouth dropped.

"What?" Soleil exclaimed.

"H-hold on," I said.

Victoria: *Dead body??*

Toby: *Yes*

CHAPTER 6

Toby

I STARED AT THE PARTIALLY-DECOMPOSED body Alex had dug up. A million questions ran through my mind. How long had it been there? Who had put it there? Why? What had led Alex to dig it up now?

The gray wolf plunked himself on the ground next to me. He could probably feel my anxiety, and with him being an unofficial part of the pack, I was his acting alpha. He felt responsible for my stress.

I reached down and rubbed his scruff. "What do you think this means?"

He let out a yelp.

"That good, huh?" I turned to Brick. "Where's Gessilyn?"

"On the phone with her parents."

My stomach twisted in knots. Gessilyn's face had paled when she saw the body. She'd spun around and run back inside almost immediately.

"Can you go find out what's going on?"

"Whatever you need, sir." He rushed inside.

I held my head higher, listening for Victoria's car. But the Bentley was so quiet, I probably wouldn't hear anything until she activated the gate to open.

Alex whined.

"What are you thinking this means?" I asked. If only we could communicate outright. It was so strange having a pack member who only turned human when the rest of us turned into wolves. So far, only Victoria had met him as a human.

Jet came over. "How long do you think it's been there?"

"I'm hardly an expert in body decomposition, but I would assume that without a casket protecting it from the bugs and the soil, it would decay faster. On the other hand, a curse could keep it in the same shape for years. Basically, I have no idea."

He leaned over and studied it. "That makes two of us."

We could only see the head and shoulders—that was as much as Alex had unearthed before howling nonstop to get our attention.

The gate opened, and Victoria drove in with Soleil. They were practically attached at the hip these days, and I couldn't have been happier—unless it was me spending all that time with her. She parked before the gate closed, and they both ran over.

"What happened?" Victoria threw her arms around me.

Soleil walked over and took a peek. "It wasn't natural causes. I can assure you of that much."

"How do you know?" Jet asked.

"Oh, I don't know." Soleil's tone dripped with sarcasm. "I'm just an angel of death."

Jet scowled. "What happened to him, then?"

"He asked too many annoying questions."

"Whatever. If you can't tell us, just say so."

Her eyes widened and she shuddered, holding her arms

tightly across her chest. "I sense dark magic—really bad stuff. It feels like it's crawling all over my skin."

"That explains why Gessilyn freaked out." Jet moved closer to the body. "Why's it here?"

Victoria clung to me all the tighter. "Should we call the police?"

I shuddered at the thought. "And give the humans more reason to distrust us? No, we'll deal with this on our own. First, we'll see what Gessilyn has to say. I might have to bring Tap into it."

"Tap?" Victoria asked. "The bartender is supposed to help with this?"

Sal came over. "He's much more than that."

"He was once a king," Soleil said.

"That's a little over the top, wouldn't you say?" Sal asked.

"No. He led his people. They may be trolls, but he led them all."

"Does that make Toby a king?" Jet folded his arms. "Before all the dead crossed over, he was the head alpha over all packs in the world."

"A lot of supernatural kings tend to be tyrannical," I said. "Neither Tap nor I have ever had any interest in that. I was more of an overseer."

Victoria stared at me, her eyes wide. "You were the alpha that the other alphas answered to?"

I glared at Jet. He had to bring that up now, didn't he?

Jet shrugged, and Victoria continued looking at me expectantly.

"It's true." I sighed. "Now isn't the time to go over the details, but yes. I started a movement of peace. There was harmony between every pack, and we even broke the ages-old vampire-werewolf hatred."

Her mouth gaped. "So, that's what a world without our fathers looks like."

"It's not quite that simple, but essentially. And once the tyrants of old returned, it took almost no time at all to destroy everything we worked so hard to build."

Victoria frowned. "I wish I could have seen it."

I kissed the top of her head. "Me, too. You'd have loved it."

Gessilyn ran out. Brick wasn't far behind.

"What's going on?" I exclaimed.

She stood tall, eying the dead body. "That's what I intend to find out."

"Black magic?" I asked.

Gessilyn nodded. "Nothing good ever comes from it."

"What does it mean?" Victoria asked.

"I'm hoping my parents can help figure that out."

The sun was quickly lowering.

I frowned. "I'm going to have to get to that card game soon."

"Really?" Jet exclaimed. "Now?"

"Am I supposed to miss the first one due to finding a body buried on our property?" I asked. "Is that going to help any of the rumors already going around?"

"I guess not."

"Look, I don't like it any more than the rest of you, but if we're going to live with the humans, we need to keep up appearances. There's no other choice. Gessilyn's on this. We've got Soleil and Tap, also.

"Victoria and I were on our way to the Faeble before you

interrupted us," Soleil said.

"You two should head over there," I said. "Let him know what's going on. Maybe he's heard something. If not, he can listen to conversation and see if anything arises."

"I can listen, too." Soleil tapped her ears. "These babies are trained in the art of eavesdropping."

"Great," Dillon muttered.

"What's taking them so long to figure it out?" My stomach tightened.

"You can always stay here," Jet said.

"How do you suggest I do that?"

"Just say you can't make it. You don't have to tell them you've got a dead body." He shrugged.

"Then I'm on the outs with some of the chattier professors." I shook my head and glanced at the time. "Maybe I can have a winning streak, and they'll want to end early."

"We'll find out if Tap knows anything," Victoria said.

"Thank you." I gave her a quick kiss. "You guys should go so you can get your homework done before your trip to Seattle tomorrow."

"Are you going to pick me up?" Ziamara asked.

Soleil shook her head. "Sorry, we can't come here—half the people going with us are human. You and I can head over together in the morning."

They discussed their plans, and I headed inside to find Gessilyn. Moonhaven was quiet. A floorboard creaked underfoot.

"Gessilyn," I called.

Where was she?

I pulled out my phone and sent her a text.

Toby: *Where ru?*

Gessilyn: *At Mother's. Looking into old manuscripts. Talk soon.*

Toby: *OK. Hurry.*

Gessilyn: *I will.*

I went back outside. Soleil, Ziamara, and Victoria were talking, outside her car.

"Are you leaving?" I asked.

"Yeah," Victoria said. "We're going to have a sleepover tonight."

"Let me know if you need anything." I wrapped my arms around her and took possession of her lips and let the kiss linger. We really needed to set a wedding date. After all these years away from her, I didn't want to be apart any longer.

She pressed herself closer and stared at me, pink covering her cheeks.

"You, too." I glanced at Ziamara. "You stay safe, too."

"What about me?" Soleil threw me a playful pout. "Don't you want me safe, too?"

I chuckled. "Somehow I'm not too worried about a valkyrie."

Soleil shrugged. "Yeah, you're right. Not too many give me a run for my money. Let's go. The later it gets, the busier Tap will be."

Victoria and I stole another kiss before climbing into our respective vehicles. My Hummer roared to life, and I put the address Roger had given me into the GPS. It wasn't too far away, at least.

I waited for Victoria and the girls to go through the gate

before going myself. I closed it and followed the directions, which led me to a sleepy-looking residential area and parked in front of the house, which had four cars in the driveway and a couple more on the curb.

The front door opened before I reached it. Roger stepped out wearing a green visor and a huge smile. "Password."

"What?"

He laughed and slapped my shoulder. "Works for me. Come on in. We're all downstairs. Did you bring anything to eat or drink?" He glanced down at my empty hands.

"I didn't realize—"

"No worries. You're the newbie. Come on in." He pulled me inside and slammed the door. "Now that we're all here, we can get started. Hope you brought some cash."

"That I did."

He led me down some stairs. "That's more important than snacks, anyway. Did you get lost or something?"

"Something came up at home."

"I don't know how you live with all those college kids." Roger shook his head. "It'd drive me nuts. Being around them all day is enough to send me to the liquor cabinet."

"We're family, and they just need a little guidance." And a witch to keep them safe from black magic.

Roger and I rounded a corner to a dimly lit room. Five of our colleagues sat around a round table, stuffing food into their mouths.

"Foley!" several exclaimed.

"Grab a seat," Roger said. "I'm going to see if the beers are ready."

"He likes to stick them in the freezer until they're just so," said Nick. He was from the math department, also.

"Nice." I took the empty seat next to him.

"You any good?" asked a guy I recognized, but couldn't think of his name.

"He teaches stats," Nick said. "We all have to watch out. He can figure out the probability of us talking smack."

"It's pretty high," said Lewis from history.

Everyone around the table roared with laughter.

Roger reappeared with an armload of bottles. He handed one to each of us. "Chilled to perfection."

Lewis shuffled a stack of cards—it looked like two decks— and dealt them.

I grabbed a handful of popcorn before checking out my hand. He'd dealt me a perfect straight.

"Newbie goes last." Roger laughed.

Nick shook his head and gave me a sympathetic glance. "He loves initiations. If you make it through tonight, you'll be one of us."

I gave Roger my fiercest stare. "Bring it on."

"See?" Roger said. "I told you he was nothing like the last guy."

Lewis busted out laughing. "I thought that poor guy was going to burst into tears."

Roger shrugged. "Wouldn't be the first time."

Nick shoved some poker chips my way and explained the values they used for each color. I grabbed some and planned my moves. As it turned out, I could've won the round, but I didn't want to find out what other initiations Roger had in mind, so I folded. I'd let them think I was just an average player for a few rounds before showing them what I was really made of. If only they'd known I'd been playing card games for far longer than any of them had been alive—even the ones with salt and pepper hair.

As the night wore on, Roger continued bringing down more chilled-to-perfection drinks. Once the chips and dip disappeared, Lewis grinned. "Time for Uncle Dan's."

"Now we bring out the good stuff." Roger got up and disappeared again.

"Is that a new beer?" I asked.

Lewis looked at me like I was crazy. "I thought you were from around here."

"I am."

"And you've never had Uncle Dan's?"

"Uncle Dan's what?" I asked, suddenly curious.

"Seriously, you've never had it?" Nick asked.

"Nope." I'd eaten unicorn horn flakes more times than I could count, but they thought I was crazy for not having... whatever it was they were talking about.

Roger came down balancing a bowl of chips and a bowl of dip.

I arched a brow. Everyone dug in, scooping out mountains of dip onto their chips.

"Hope you mixed up a second batch this time," Lewis said, scooping out more.

"Yep." Roger glanced at me. "Try some. You're not officially a Northwesterner until you've had Uncle Dan's dip."

"Okay." I grabbed a curved chip and scooped a little of the white dip.

"Come on," Nick said. "You need more."

"All right." I took as much as the others had. They all

watched in eager expectation. I took a bite. The thick, creamy dip sent an explosion of tastes through my mouth. It was kind of like ranch, only so much better. I reached for more.

"See?"

"Now you can say you're from here."

"The new guy likes it!"

"It's like crack," Roger said. "Once you start, there's no stopping."

I laughed, glad I'd decided to join the game. It was fun to get away from all the worries back at Moonhaven for a while. Plus, now I had a new food to introduce to the pack.

Lewis handed me the stack of cards. "You're dealer this round."

We laughed and played for a few hours, and I left with about twenty more dollars in my pocket than when I'd started. To my relief, there were no actual initiations.

As I climbed into the Hummer, the joy from the evening slipped away. What was going on at Moonhaven with the dead body?

CHAPTER 7

Victoria

"MAYBE WE SHOULD GET DOWN to the car," Sasha said. "Looks like we're almost there." She'd been eager to get off the ferry since the moment it disembarked.

I finished off my coffee and glanced out the window. "We're still a little ways off. I want to go out onto the deck again."

Sasha covered her mouth. "I'm going to the car. See you guys there."

"Poor thing." Jacey, one of our Waldensian house mates, frowned. She fluffed her long, layered black hair. "I'd go with her, but I want to go on the deck with you. Does that make me awful?"

"No," said Cheyenne, Jacey's roommate. "I'll go down with her."

"Thanks." I smiled at her. "I just need to stretch my legs."

Jacey and I went out to the deck, where Soleil and Ziamara stood, watching the water as their hair flapped around in the breeze.

"Where's everyone else?" Soleil asked. "Don't tell me I scared them away."

Jacey laughed. "Hardly. Poor Sasha is totally seasick."

"Oh," Soleil said. "I can—"

I shot her a glare.

She rolled her eyes at me. "—see if they sell any medicine inside."

"Would it do any good at this point?" Jacey glanced toward the land, which was rapidly approaching.

Soleil shrugged. "I wouldn't know. Never been green on a boat."

Ziamara pulled her rainbow hair into a bun. "Must be awful. I love being out here—I couldn't imagine it making me nauseated."

The speakers behind us crackled, and then the captain announced it was time to return to the vehicles.

We made our way down to Sasha's Highlander. She had the driver's seat reclined and Cheyenne sat next to her. The rest of us climbed in the back.

"Are we there yet?" Sasha moaned.

"Just about," Jacey reassured her.

"Do you want me to drive?" I asked. "You look like you could use a break."

"Maybe. Let's see if I feel better once the floor stops moving."

"I'd have suggested driving around if I knew you get seasick," I said.

"Me, too."

"Let's get our minds off it," Soleil said. She reached into the front and turned up the music.

Sasha groaned.

"Maybe you *should* let someone else drive," Cheyenne said.

"No, I'm fine." Sasha put the seat upright and clutched the steering wheel. "See? Better already."

Ziamara and I exchanged doubtful expressions.

By the time we drove off the ferry and onto land, Sasha was singing to the music and joking. She still looked a little green, but nowhere near as bad as before.

"You know how to get to the Space Needle?" Jacey asked.

"Nope," Sasha said.

"What time's our lunch reservation?" I asked.

"Reservations?" Cheyenne asked.

"We can't just show up?" asked Sasha.

"Guess we'll find out." I shrugged.

Someone's stomach rumbled. Everyone laughed, but no one took credit for it.

Once we got on the freeway, traffic barely moved.

"Should we stop and eat somewhere else?" Jacey asked. "I don't care if we eat up there or not."

"It's the Space Needle," Cheyenne whined. "My parents got engaged there. I can't come to the city without going there."

"You don't have to tell them," Jacey pointed out.

Soleil and I exchanged an amused glance. It was really nice to get away and not have to worry about anything more than seasickness or where to eat.

Cheyenne turned and looked at us. "You guys want to have lunch six hundred feet above ground, right?"

Sasha moaned again. "I hope I don't get sick."

"It's not floating in water."

"And it might be after three before we get there." Sasha blared her horn at someone who cut her off. "Yeah, back at you, pal."

We finally made it off the freeway and to the Seattle Center. As we drove around, looking for a place to park, we passed the needle. It had a line wrapped around it.

"Is that for the restaurant?" Ziamara asked.

"Please can we just eat somewhere else?" Jacey begged. "We can go up the elevator later, Chey. Then you can tell your parents you were there. We can walk on the deck and everything."

"Fine." Cheyenne sighed. "Let's just eat at the courtyard, but we're not leaving until I've been to the top of the needle."

We all agreed. My stomach was rumbling, and I would have agreed to eat just about anything.

After we got out of the car, Ziamara pulled me aside. "Do you smell that?"

I sniffed. "Werewolves. They're not too far away."

"They smell different."

"Probably mutts."

"Mutts?" Ziamara asked.

"Humans turned from being bitten," I said.

"Really?" she asked. "I didn't even know that was possible."

"It's usually frowned upon," I said. "And by that, I mean punishable by death in most packs."

Ziamara flinched. "That's harsh." She'd been born human and turned into a vampire.

"That's also why Toby is so against the traditional ways and refuses to follow them. Just about everything is punishable by death." I shuddered, thinking back to my own death—all because Toby and I wanted to marry each other. Death was definitely the preferred option when my other choice was marrying that tyrant, Franklin, who had always looked at me like I was a servant and puppy factory.

Sasha turned around. "What are you guys doing? Come on!"

The three of us hurried over to them. The mutt smell lingered, almost like we were following it. Or they were following us.

I shook my head. That was ridiculous. Some newly-turned wolves were probably just hanging out.

We all got food at the courtyard and took it outside. It was chilly, but sunny.

"Where are we going shopping?" Jacey asked.

Sasha shot me a knowing glance. "We're finding a cute bag for Victoria. I don't know how you can carry around that backpack."

"It's convenient." I shrugged and bit into my burger.

"You're hopeless," Sasha said. "I don't get how you can be so stylish in practically every other way, and then not care about your bag. I mean, really. You may as well just throw on any old pair of ugly shoes."

Cheyenne gasped. "Now that's just mean."

A new werewolf scent drifted our way. Ziamara and I exchanged a worried glance. It wasn't a mutt. In fact, it smelled eerily close to my pack of origin—the very ones who felt I'd betrayed them. They wanted me dead.

I choked on a fry.

"You okay?" Sasha's eyes widened.

Soleil whacked me on the back, somehow helping to dislodge the food.

"I'm fine." I would be unless someone dragged me to my father.

"Where do we want to go next?" Cheyenne asked.

While they discussed shopping, I scanned the periphery. Nothing looked out of place, but then again, everyone in the pack probably dressed in modern clothes, making it all that much harder to spot them in a crowd.

"Does that sound good?" Jacey asked. "Victoria?"

I snapped my attention back to my friends. "Uh, yeah. Whatever you guys want to do."

Soleil arched a brow. "You okay?"

"Couldn't be better."

She frowned, obviously knowing the truth.

I looked away. "Let's shop 'til we drop!"

Sasha and Cheyenne squealed, and then we all threw our trash away. We wandered around, not finding much in the way of shops.

Jacey frowned. "Now what? Go downtown? To the waterfront?"

"First, we go to the needle." Cheyenne stared her down. "I love shopping as much as the next girl, but I came for the restaurant."

Sasha sighed like someone asked her to move the famous landmark across town. "Fine. Let's go."

We turned around and headed the other way. I stopped near the enormous water fountain. Even with it being so cold, kids ran around the edge, getting sprayed by the mist.

The scent of my old pack tickled my nose. Someone was nearby.

"This is pretty and all," Cheyenne said, "but can we get going? I—"

"Shh." I focused on the smell, trying to tell what direction it came from. There was a slight circular breeze, making it hard to tell.

"Cute guy?" Jacey looked in the direction I faced.

Then I saw him. Tall, muscular, and shaggy hair. He wore an all-too-familiar brown leather jacket.

He stepped out from behind a large tree and leaned against it, looking deep in thought. Maybe he didn't recognize my scent, or maybe the breeze was keeping it from him.

"Let's go," Cheyenne said.

"Oh, I see him now," Jacey said. "Wow, he's hot. Good eye, Victoria."

There was nothing attractive about *that* man. He was a cruel, horrible werewolf. One I could never forget if I died a thousand deaths.

Had he tracked me, or was it bad luck?

"You wanna go say hi?" Sasha asked.

"No." I couldn't pull my gaze away from him.

"Do you know him?" Soleil asked.

I swallowed. "His name is Franklin."

My pulse pounded in my ears. Franklin would want me dead every bit as much as my father did. I'd been pledged to marry him, but I'd run off to be with Toby. I'd humiliated him, and to an arrogant wolf, that was the worst thing you could do. Even with as many years that had passed, his wrath would be as fresh as the night I'd run away.

He turned my way.

CHAPTER 8

Victoria

TERROR TORE THROUGH ME. THE scent of fear was stronger than any other. It would reach him in a matter of moments.

I had to make a decision—quickly. If I stayed with my friends, I would put them in danger.

There was no other choice. I had to run.

"Victoria?" Sasha asked.

My mouth went dry. I spun around and ran, careful to stay at the speed of humans so as not to attract any unnecessary attention. With all my senses on high alert, I could hear my friends confused exclamations.

Another thing I heard—footsteps. Heavy and fast. Franklin's scent grew stronger as he closed the distance between us.

I glanced over my shoulder. He'd already passed the fountain. Soleil and Ziamara ran to block him, but he darted around them.

Why had I agreed to come on this trip? I should have been studying safely in the library—or better yet, at Moonhaven.

I ran into someone.

"Hey, watch it!"

"Sorry." I turned my attention in front of me and pushed

my legs to go as quickly as possible, not caring who saw me run so fast.

Franklin's odor continued growing stronger.

I darted down between two buildings. Trash bags lay scattered along the tight walkway. I jumped over some and ran around others.

"Stop!"

"Never."

His hand brushed my coat. I held in a scream and forced myself to move faster. A dumpster blocked my path, giving me only a few inches to get past. I pressed myself against the wall and squeezed by.

"There's no point in running," he grunted.

"Just leave me alone. I already died for what I did."

He reached for me. "But I didn't get to do it."

I made it past the dumpster and continued down the tight alleyway. Hopefully, I would come to an exit rather than a dead end.

Franklin grabbed the fabric and pulled. My coat's collar squeezed my neck and my heart raced all the more.

"You know, I've always loved the aroma of your fear."

I kicked backward, but it wasn't enough to loosen his grip. A low growl escaped my throat. I spun around and spit in his face.

"You're going to regret that." He let go and wiped his face. His eyes widened as he realized his mistake.

I turned around and ran, gasping for air. "No, I'd do it again."

I rounded a corner and an opening appeared. Renewed with hope, I picked up speed.

My foot caught on something. I stumbled, trying to regain my footing. Seriously, I had to be the world's clumsiest wolf. Maybe that was it! What if it had something to do with not being able to shift? Clearly, that was something to look into later—assuming I could get away from Franklin.

He grabbed my hair and yanked my head backward.

I cried out in pain.

"That's better."

"Let go!" I fought to spin around, but he pinned my left arm behind my back.

"Now we're going to set some things right."

"Never." I struggled to get away.

Franklin simultaneously yanked my hair harder and shoved his elbow into my spine. "That's what you think."

"What do you think you're going to do?"

"I'm taking what's rightfully mine. Now play nice." He stared at me with his muddy brown eyes.

Did he really think I would give up that easily? I continued struggling against him.

He forced me out of the alley. We were still between buildings, and no one was within sight.

Since I couldn't get away, that left me with only one choice. It was a risky one, but I had to take it. I took a deep breath and stared up at the sky. I struggled to find my inner wolf. She was growing weaker with each shift we missed.

I focused on a cloud and howled.

Franklin laughed. "You think that's going to help? Our pack rules this part of town. No werewolf in the area would dare cross us."

"*Our* pack?" I scoffed.

"Like it or not, that's where you belong. I haven't married yet—"

"That's no surprise." I elbowed him with my free arm.

He shoved me against a wall, pressing my cheek into freshly-chewed gum. I kicked him as hard as I could, wishing I'd thought to wear boots with a thick heel. "Watch your mouth, woman. Your father's pledge is still valid."

"Actually, I'm pretty sure my death nullified it."

"Except that you're back to life. You need to declare your submission to me."

My skin bristled. If I accepted him as my superior, nature wouldn't allow me to back out of it as long as we both lived. A wolf declaring him or herself allegiant to an alpha couldn't be undone.

He pressed my face harder against the wall. "Say it."

"Never."

"The more you fight it, the greater my victory when you finally surrender."

I gritted my teeth and kicked as high as I could, aiming for his groin.

Franklin let out a yelp. "Don't hinder your chances of having pups."

"I'm not." I aimed for the same place again.

He moved to the side, loosening his hold on my arm.

I jumped away from him, but he still had a hold on my hair. My head yanked back again. I twisted around and lunged for him, scratching his face.

His eyes narrowed and his nostrils flared. "Now you've done it."

"You think I'm done?" I exclaimed. The narcissistic tyrant

still had my hair. Fury tore through me as I lunged for him again, this time biting into his cheek.

Franklin cried out in pain, but still wouldn't let go. I bit harder and kneed him in the stomach. Finally, he let go of me and shoved me away. My back and head hit the brick wall.

I jumped back and spit blood and flesh from my mouth. He wiped blood from his eyes, smearing it along his face and sleeve. Anger burned all through me, running through me like a locomotive flying down a hill without brakes. Memories ran through my mind—things he and my father did over the years. Killing Elsie. Using force to control me and others.

"Give my father a message." I spit again.

He glared at me. "That you're crazy?"

"No, that this is just a warning. Anyone who comes after me again will get far worse."

"That's what you think. You're the one who hasn't seen nothing yet." He started to push himself up.

I spun around and ran, not about to give him another chance to go after me. The smell of my pack—my *old* pack—grew stronger. Others were nearby. It was only a matter of time before more came after me. I needed to get back to my friends right away.

Sniffing the air, I couldn't find a trace of any of them. The werewolf smell was too strong.

Had I thought ahead, I'd have brought along some wolfsbane to cover my own scent.

Fear struck me, but then I focused on the anger. How dare they continue to pursue me? I'd already made my decision to walk away, and not only that, but like I'd pointed out to Franklin, I'd paid the price. Unfortunately, that wasn't good enough for them. They would never forgive me for my decision. If I died and returned five times, they would set out to make me pay five times.

Once I broke free of the alleyways, I ran my hands through my tangled hair and jogged back to where I'd last seen the others.

They were gone.

My heart sank. Somewhere along the way, I'd lost my purse. That meant that not only did I have no way to contact my friends, but would I need to return to where Franklin had fought me. My heart raced.

Everything in my purse could be replaced. I couldn't face him again. Not right now. My face felt swollen and was throbbing. It was also getting increasingly hard to walk as pain increased in my calf and my neck ached from being yanked backward so hard.

I just wanted Toby, but he was all the way back at Moonhaven. They had their own problems trying to figure out why that body had been buried and had traces of black magic.

Exhausted, I stumbled over to a tree and leaned against the bark. The werewolf scent was farther away. Hopefully, that meant they were all moving on. With any luck, Franklin would tell them I was crazy and that they should all just leave me alone. Surely, they had to have other things to focus on—things far more important than me.

What I needed was to figure out where my friends had gone. Would they have gone to the needle? Or would they have followed me? I'd been running at supernatural speed, so they wouldn't have been able to keep up—not unless Soleil or Ziamara had also ran faster than our human friends could see.

But if they'd done that, wouldn't they have shown up and fought along with me?

My best bet was to find my purse. Then I could at least call someone. I had all of their numbers in my new phone.

I sniffed the air again and checked the direction of the breeze. My pack's smell had definitely faded, and it wasn't because the wind was blowing it in the other direction.

Stomach twisting, I went back the same way I'd gone when running from Franklin. I couldn't remember where I'd lost my handbag, but with any luck, Franklin hadn't found it.

As I ran, I wracked my mind, trying to think if anything in my purse pointed toward Moonhaven. The only thing that did was on my phone behind a complicated password they wouldn't be able to guess easily.

My leg continued aching the farther I walked. I started to limp. I managed to get back to the alley, though. My stomach lurched as I stared down it.

"Are you okay, Miss?" came a masculine voice from behind.

I spun around, ready to fight.

It was just a police officer, and he smelled thoroughly human. My body relaxed.

"What happened to your face?" he asked. "Do you need medical attention?"

I shook my head. "I lost my purse. I need to get it."

"Let me look at your eye." He reached for my face, and I flinched. "What happened?"

"I was attacked."

"By whom?"

My nostrils flared. "A psychopath."

"Let me call for an ambulance."

"No." I shook my head furiously, but stopped as the pain grew worse.

A look of concern washed over the officer's face. "You need medical attention. Come with me."

"My purse!"

"I'll send someone to find it." He pulled out a walkie-talkie and spoke into it, directing someone to send medics our way.

While he was distracted, I bolted down the alleyway. If Franklin hadn't grabbed my purse, I needed to, before someone else did. Though already starting to heal, my leg gave out and I crashed onto the hard concrete.

Footsteps sounded as the officer came after me. "You're a determined one. Do you know where you dropped it?"

I pulled myself to sitting. "Down this way. I don't remember exactly."

"Did the perpetrator take it?"

"I don't know. That wasn't what he was after."

He arched a brow. "Why did he attack you, then?"

That was a loaded question.

The officer stared at me expectantly.

"He thinks I should marry him."

He nodded knowingly. "Domestic disputes can get ugly fast. Let's get you out there, where the medics can find us easier."

I sighed, giving in. I'd have a hard time explaining how I healed quickly because of being a werewolf, but at least I wouldn't be anywhere the pack could get to me.

The officer helped me out of the alley, and as soon as we made it out, two medics came running around the corner. His walkie-talkie buzzed and then a lady spoke in code. He turned to the medics. "I have to go—robbery in progress. She needs to give a statement before being released. She was attacked."

"Understood."

The officer turned to me. "They'll take care of you." He ran off.

"My purse." I pointed down the alleyway.

"You lost it down there?" asked one of the medics, a man with graying hair and deep lines around his eyes and mouth.

I nodded.

He turned to the younger guy. "You check her out. I'll look for her purse."

I might have a hard time explaining my quick healing, but at least my old pack couldn't get to me now.

CHAPTER 9

Toby

I PACED THE LENGTH OF THE field as Gessilyn and her family studied the body. They had been circled around it for hours.

Sal came over to me. "Let's get some lunch, sir."

"No. Something's wrong. I can feel it."

"The black magic is getting to everyone. I think the longer you stay out here, the more it gets to us."

I scowled. Something from the pit of my stomach told me that trouble lurked close by.

"Food will do you good."

"How?" I snapped.

A hurt expression covered his face, but it disappeared as quickly as it had come.

"I didn't mean to snap, Sal. I know you're just trying to help."

He nodded. "It's getting to all of us."

"How much longer are they going to need?"

Sal shrugged. "As long as it takes, I suppose. Gessilyn is nothing if not thorough. They want to get to the bottom of this as much as you do."

My stomach twisted in tight knots.

"Come on inside. Pacing isn't going to help you any."

He was right. "At least it helps me blow off some steam."

I pulled out my phone and checked the time. It was well past lunchtime, and not a text or call from Victoria. I hoped that meant she was having fun. At least she wasn't here, dealing with all the stress.

"You're stressing the pack out," Sal said. He glanced toward the house, and I followed his gaze. Several of the guys had their faces pressed against windows.

"All right. Let's head inside." I doubted my stomach would let me eat, but I could try to calm everyone else's nerves.

As soon as we walked through the front door, the aroma of Brick's famous stew greeted us. My mouth watered, but my insides continued twisting together.

"Hey, boss," Brick called. "Heard from the girls yet?"

"Nope. They're probably having too much fun shopping to think about us."

"I'm glad someone is," he said. "Come and eat. You need the fuel."

Dillon charged down the stairs. "Any news on that body?"

I shook my head, unable to shake the feeling that something was horribly wrong. "The witches still haven't found anything."

He grumbled and went to the kitchen table. I followed him and we sat in silence.

Brick set bowls in front of each of them. "Eat up. I made plenty."

My stomach relented, giving into the savory meal. I'd downed three large bowls before finishing.

"I told you that you needed to eat," Sal said, with a hint of teasing in his tone.

"You were right." I couldn't bring myself to be playful, though.

"And you look better, too," Brick said.

"I need to go to the Faeble and talk with Tap. Maybe he's heard something."

Jet came in. "I'll go with. I need a drink—something strong, and preferably with unicorn horn flakes."

"Everything okay?" I asked.

He shook his head. "I can't reach Ziamara."

My head snapped to attention. "What?"

"She's not answering her phone."

I turned to Brick. "You haven't heard from Soleil, either, have you?"

Pink crept into the burly werewolf's cheeks. "She hardly has to check in with me."

"Yeah, but you two talk all the time, right?"

Brick turned back to the stew. "You should go talk with Tap. That troll hears everything."

I ran my hands through my hair, pulling tight. "Yeah. Anyone else going?"

Everyone else shook their heads.

"Guess it's just you and me," Jet said.

"Looks like it."

He twisted his head to the left, making his neck crack. "I can't tell you how much I wish we could turn at will. I hate being stuck in this slow form."

"Tell me about it." I glanced outside at the circle of witches around the dead body. "Unfortunately, other things take precedence."

Jet muttered something under his breath.

"I'm sure the guy out there isn't too happy, either."

"Let's just go. I want to hear what Tap has to say."

"You and me both." I glanced at Brick. "If anyone hears from the ladies, call us right away."

"Will do, sir."

I sighed as we made our way outside.

"Are you worried about them, too?" Jet asked.

"Yes, but I'm sure they're fine. The body and the dark magic is probably getting the best of us. They're probably having the time of their lives."

"I hope you're right."

It bothered me that we both had our concerns, but with everything going on, it made sense our nerves were on edge.

"Maybe we should ask another witch to look into breaking the curse of the moon," Jet said as we jogged through the thick woods.

"Others have, and they've all failed," I said. "Each and every one of them. Gessilyn and her family are our best bet."

"When's that going to happen? Seems like things keep coming up."

"Figuring out why Victoria can't shift is more important. The rest of us aren't in any danger because of the curse. It would be more convenient if we could choose when to shift, but we can't."

"I know that. I'm not saying she shouldn't be the priority over breaking the curse, but think about this. What if by breaking the moon's curse, she's finally able to turn along with the rest of us? The general moon curse might break her individual curse, too."

I paused, considering and then doubting the theory. "It's possible, but it's not a risk I'm willing to take. She needs to let her wolf out as soon as possible. The rest of us can wait—we've waited this long."

"But—"

"I'm done discussing it, Jet. As soon as Victoria's safe—and she's not now while she's unable to turn—then we'll focus our priorities."

He cleared his throat. "I understand. Will you give me permission to find someone else who can try to help us out with the curse?"

"Someone better than the high witch and her family?" I grew irritated. "No, and I need you to drop it. That dead body could be a curse, now unleashed. It's the only reason Gessilyn is pausing her search for Victoria's personal curse."

"But Ziamara has connections. She—"

A low growl rumbled from my throat. "I asked you to back off. I have the same connections she does with the vampire queen, but vampires aren't witches."

"I'm talking about the dragons. They have their own breed of magic, and their own system of high witches."

"And from what I understand, they've burned some bridges. Drop it."

"You won't consider it? Really?"

"Jet, when you agreed to join my pack, you chose to accept my leadership. Just because I'm for peace and against the traditional ruling structure of packs doesn't mean I'm going to be a pushover. I'm still alpha. If it turns out you can't accept that, perhaps you should consider returning home." It pained me to say it, but I couldn't deal with the constant power struggles of a born-alpha as my second-in-command.

"You and I both know I can't go back. Not after turning down my position as alpha. My younger brother would never give it up, and besides, they won't accept a vampire into the pack."

"So, you'll respect my leadership?" I stopped and turned to him.

He skidded to a stop and stared at me. "I already do. I'm just asking you to consider something else. The dragons live in their own underground world that contains a magic of its own."

"Yes, I'm aware of their cities. They, too, have had their own restructuring of leadership since death's doors opened up and released so many."

His eyes widened. "Wait."

I groaned. "What now? My patience is wearing thin."

"That body couldn't have been there very long, right? Not with the other side having opened so recently."

A headache formed at the base of my skull. I rubbed the back of my neck. "No one rose from their graves. They stepped out from one side to the other. And again, we're dealing with black magic. I'm going to talk with Tap. You can either come with me, or you can go back to the house. We're not bringing in vampires or dragons at this point. Understood?"

He scowled. "Yes."

I narrowed my eyes. "I'm serious, Yamamoto."

Jet flinched at being called by his last name.

"If you go behind my back, you're going to have to explain to your wife why you two are moving out."

"Will you think about it?"

I took a deep breath. "I'm going to the Faeble. Maybe you should go home and think hard about what you want from life."

"I'm going with you."

"Okay." I made a mental note to keep an eye on him. Turning to any other species wasn't a box I was prepared to open yet. We already had enough on our plate, and I didn't want to add in anything to complicate the situation. Although, if Victoria didn't turn soon, I might have no other choice except to turn to anyone available. One of the vampire queen's daughters had married a dragon king, and Jet was right about that species having a magic all its own.

We ran the rest of the way to the supernatural bar in silence. The scents of other creatures grew stronger as we neared it. My body relaxed with each step toward the building. Tap would know what to do. The tough little troll who'd stepped down from his own role of leadership to run the bar was a wealth of knowledge not only because of how old he was, but because of the great number of supernaturals he talked to on a given day.

Jet and I went around the little building to the entrance. Bright lights and loud music greeted us. One of the main rooms was full of teenagers dancing and eating.

I went over to the bar and took a seat. Tap and Quinn ran around, busily making drinks, not seeming to notice my presence. Jet sat next to me.

"Did we come at a bad time?" I asked.

Tap turned to me with a harried expression. "A djinn is having her sweet sixteen."

"Though it's anything but sweet," Quinn added. "They're

as wild as any creature comes."

"And thirsty." Tap added another drink to a round tray and handed it to Quinn. "Take this over. I'll work on the next round."

"Maybe we should come back," I said.

Jet shot me a look that said he thought I was crazy. "I'm not letting some blood-thirsty, teenage genies push us out of here."

I snorted. Djinn were hardly genies—at least not in the popular sense of the word. They looked just like anyone else, but as soon as they needed their powers, their skin turned purple and spiky.

"I'll get to you two," Tap told Jet, pouring some faerie dust into a purple, sparkly drink. "Just give me a minute. I need to get their orders first. The last thing I want is an angry djinn."

"Can't you make them grant you wishes?" Jet asked.

"Human myth," Tap said. "You'll never see a genie in a bottle, kid. These creatures live in caves and have a poisonous touch." He shuddered.

"They're that deadly?" Jet asked, eying the party.

"A djinn's poison is worse than death—unless you can escape." Tap added the last drink to the tray and hurried away.

Quinn came back a moment later. "They're crazy! A couple started flirting with me. One nearly touched me!"

Jet arched a brow. "What would happen if they did?"

Quinn came over to the bar and leaned over it, whispering. "They'll turn your mind into an alternate reality. It's almost impossible to escape without outside help. There are rumors of people dragged into their caves, spending centuries in their own minds, believing that they're living out their worst nightmares."

"And Tap lets them in?" Jet exclaimed.

"These ones are supposed to be good, only using their poison against evildoers." Quinn scrunched his face. "I can't say that I trust them." He stood up tall and spoke in a normal tone. "What can I get you two?"

"How about out of here?" Jet muttered.

I rolled my eyes. "I'll have that rainbow glitter drink that Soleil likes."

Jet snickered. "Turning soft?"

"Don't knock it 'til you try it."

"Some other time."

Quinn turned to Jet. "What do you want?"

Jet glanced over at the djinns. "The strongest thing you have."

"Coming right up." He turned around and started mixing the drinks.

Tap came over and stood up on his platform to make him appear taller. "I think that'll hold them for a little while. What's on your mind, Toby?"

"That obvious?" I asked.

He chuckled. "I can read you like a book, my friend. Still trying to find that cure for Victoria?"

I nodded. "But that's not the worst of it. We've got a dead body on my property."

"Oh?" Tap asked.

"It's shrouded in black magic."

The troll's eyes widened and his face paled.

My stomach twisted tighter than before. "What?" But I wasn't sure I wanted to know.

Tap opened his mouth, but before he could speak, Soleil ran around the corner, her eyes wild.

"What are you doing here?" I exclaimed. "Aren't you supposed to be in Seattle?"

"We have a problem."

CHAPTER 10

Toby

I STARED BACK AND FORTH between Soleil and Tap, both of whom had horrified expressions.

"You first," I told Soleil.

She pulled hair behind her ears and swallowed. "Don't freak out, but—"

"I think you just assured he will," Jet said.

Soleil glared at him. "Shut it, would you?" She turned to me and glanced at Tap before looking at me. "Like I said, don't freak."

"I'm going to if you don't tell me!"

"Victoria's missing."

My mouth dropped open.

"What do you mean by 'missing'?" Tap asked.

My mind spun, trying to make sense of it. "Did she wander off? Was she kidnapped?"

Soleil twisted hair around a finger. "She and Ziamara smelled werewolf. Then something spooked Victoria, and she bolted. She was already out of sight before I realized what happened. We all ran after her, but the city is a big place."

"Is Ziamara safe?" Jet sprung off his stool.

"Yeah. She's with the other girls. They were going to keep looking, and then report Victoria's disappearance to the police."

The room spun around me. I'd just gotten her back, and now she was gone? Once she returned, I was never going to let her out of my sight again. Ever. I pulled myself from the stool.

"Do you know anything about the werewolf?" Tap asked.

Soleil shook her head. "I never saw him."

"You couldn't smell him?" Jet asked.

She shook her head. "That's not how I work."

"How exactly do you work?" I asked.

"I drink people's essence, remember? That's how I find out most everything I need to know. I can sense things like black magic, but I can't tell what different species *smell* like. You're the canines, remember?"

I frowned. "We have to find Victoria. What if one of our old packs found her?"

"I know you're worried about Victoria," Tap said, "but I need to tell you what I know about the body."

"What?" I sat back down.

"You said black magic is involved?" Tap asked.

I nodded, unable to speak.

"And the body has been unearthed?"

"Not completely," Jet said. "Our wolfborn found him."

"You picked up a wolfborn?" Tap asked.

"What's the news about the body?" I snapped.

Tap crossed his arms. "You've been cursed."

My eyes nearly popped from my head. "All of us?"

"Anyone who's been on the property."

Glass broke in the next room.

"I'd better check on those djinn." Quinn scrambled out of sight.

"How do you know we've been cursed?" Soleil asked. "There are different kinds of black magic."

"And yet some signs are universal."

Quinn returned. "They need more drinks."

Tap spun around and grabbed a couple glasses.

"Does Gessilyn know?" Jet asked.

"I'm sure she would've told us if she did." I turned to Soleil. "Take me to Seattle."

"Me, too," Jet said.

"No." I shook my head. "You're going back to Moonhaven and telling Gessilyn that we've been cursed."

Jet's nostrils flared. "My wife is over there, too."

We stared each other down.

Soleil muttered something about the pride of alphas. "I can only take one of you, anyway."

I turned from Jet and arched a brow at the angel of death. "What do you mean?"

"Some might call it teleporting."

Jet swore. "Seriously? You can do that?"

"It weakens me—especially when I bring someone with me—so I don't do it often. I might need to drink some of your essence, Toby."

"Fine, whatever it takes to get to Victoria. Can't you just travel to where she is?"

"That'd be nice, but no, I can't. Not unless I know *where* she is. That's why I've been given over a decade to find that dictator I'm supposed to kill."

"How's the search going, by the way?" Jet asked.

A growl escaped my lips. "Just get to Moonhaven. Call me as soon as you hear *anything*."

"You, too. I need to know Zia's okay."

"She is." Soleil turned to me. "Let's make like a bread truck and haul buns."

I turned to Tap. "Do you know of anyone who can help us with either the body or finding Victoria?"

"I know some people. Let me take care of the party first, and then I'll see what I can do. Otherwise, I might not be any use to you if I tick off a hormonal djinn."

"Thanks, Tap. I'll keep my phone on me." I glanced at Soleil. "Right?"

"Yep. Everything comes with you. No embarrassing wardrobe malfunctions when you travel with me."

"Good to know." I glanced at Jet. "Moonhaven."

"Leaving now." He finished his drink and left.

I turned to Soleil. "How do we do this?"

"Out in the woods. It's too loud here." She grabbed my drink and finished it off. "Thanks."

"Wait," I said. "Maybe we should go back to Moonhaven and see if Gessilyn can run a locator spell. Wouldn't that be better than running all over a major city, looking for Victoria?"

"Gessilyn needs to focus on the body," Tap said. "Victoria's your mate. You can sniff her out from a greater distance."

"Unless someone rubbed wolfsbane all over her," I grumbled.

My phone rang. It played a love song—it was from Victoria's new number. My heart skipped a beat.

I reached for the phone, and it slid from my hand as I

pulled it from my pocket. It fell to the ground and slid across the floor, landing under a table full of patrons. I jumped after it and crawled under the table, bumping into feet.

"Hey, watch it!"

"What do you think you're doing?"

"Get outta here."

My fingers wrapped around the still-ringing phone and I climbed out from under the table without apology. With shaking hands, I managed to answer it.

"Hello? Victoria?"

Dead air.

"Victoria!"

Nothing.

I looked at my phone. The screen was blank. I turned it on and found Victoria in my contacts list and called her back.

No answer.

"Why?" I cried.

Soleil came over and helped me up.

I tried calling her back again, but again no answer.

"Why isn't she answering? She *just* called."

"Or someone found her phone. We don't know anything."

"I have to call her back."

"Let's go outside."

"She just called. That song only plays when it's her." I called Victoria again.

Nothing, again.

Soleil put an arm around me and guided me toward the exit. "We should get to Seattle."

"Wait!" Tap waved us over to the bar.

I turned to him, calling Victoria again.

"Come closer," he said.

We went back to where we'd been sitting.

He lowered his voice and leaned across the counter. "I do know of someone who can help with a locator spell since Gessilyn is busy."

"Who?" I put my phone away.

Tap glanced around to make sure no one was listening. "He has a store just outside of campus. The cover is a spice shop, but he's an apothecary of sorts. He can concoct medicines and such."

"You mean spells," Soleil said.

"Yes, but he doesn't work with just anyone." Tap grabbed a paper and scribbled a note. "Give this to him, so he knows I sent you."

"Can't you just call?" she asked.

"He's extremely old-fashioned. What else would you expect from someone whose cover is a spice shop?" Tap handed me the paper. "Just give him this, and you should be in."

I stuffed the note in my pocket next to the phone. "Anything else we need to know? What's his name?"

"Just give him the note, and he'll introduce himself."

"Do you have an exact address?" Soleil asked. "Or are we supposed to just look for a spice shop? Not that there are likely to be many."

"*I'm* not old-fashioned. I'll text it to you. Hurry, now. He closes soon."

Soleil grabbed my arm.

"Thanks," I called to Tap.

"Are we going to teleport?" I asked once we were outside.

"Not to town. It takes too much out of me, and I already

used that magic getting here."

"Hold on. Is Ziamara going to be okay? How long have you been away?"

"She promised me she'd stay with the girls."

"Can you call her?" I asked. "I'm going to keep trying Victoria."

"Sure." She pulled out her phone. "Oh, looky. Tap already texted me the address."

"Good. How close to campus?"

"Maybe a mile away."

I dialed Victoria again. No answer.

"Why won't she pick up? She just called."

"Maybe someone found her phone and is going through her contacts."

"But why not answer?" I exclaimed.

"Who knows? Or the battery could be dead."

"Let's just get over to that shop. I hope they sell restorative tea—then I won't have to drink anyone's essence."

"I thought you liked doing that," I said.

"Tea's a lot simpler. Let's pick up our speed, wolfy."

I stuck my phone back in my pocket and jogged through the woods with Soleil barely keeping up. "Are you okay?"

"Yeah." She gasped for air.

"No, you're not." I stopped. "Drink my essence—just enough to give you energy, but not enough to hurt me."

She leaned against a tree. "I never take too much. Not unless I mean to."

"Just hurry. Tap said that place closes soon." I closed my eyes and let my mouth gape open. A breeze rustled my hair as her enormous wings sprung out. Then it felt like she was pulling something silky from deep within me. My mouth opened wider on its own, and the silkiness came out with more force. I forgot where we were and why we were there. My body relaxed to the point of feeling like my bones had turned to rubber.

With a jolt, everything stopped. My body slunk toward the ground, but I caught myself and steadied my legs. Once I felt in complete control over myself, I opened my eyes. Soleil's eyes were an electric green and she appeared in a daze—much like I felt.

She blinked a few times and turned to me. "Thanks. I needed that."

"No problem. Let's get to that apothecary."

"Right." She shook her head and burst into a run.

"Hey!" I ran after her. We made it out of the woods before long.

"We should've gone to Moonhaven," I said, feeling like an idiot. "Then we could've taken the Hummer."

She pulled out her phone. "We're not far, anyway. Tap just texted me again. His buddy closes shop in fifteen minutes."

My eyes widened. "Can we make it in time?"

"There's only one way to find out."

Of course there was. My muscles were already growing tired, but this was for Victoria, so they would have to deal with it.

Soleil stepped toward the street and waved. A yellow cab pulled up to the curb.

We climbed in and Soleil gave the cabbie the address.

He grinned. "Old Willy's Spice Shop, right?"

I exchanged a curious glance with Soleil.

The cabbie pulled back into the street. "Old Willy and my pops go way back. Wow, the stories he would tell me." He chuckled.

Soleil arched a brow at me. I shrugged.

A few minutes later, the cab screeched to a halt. "The fare's on me. Just tell them Eamon says hi."

"Sure," I said. "Thanks so much."

We climbed out and hurried to the door. The short, stocky man in overalls inside the shop was turning a sign over from *Open* to *Closed*.

"Wait!" Soleil and I cried in unison.

CHAPTER 11

Toby

THE SHOP DOOR OPENED JUST a crack. "We're closed. Come back tomorrow."

I shoved my foot in the door's gap. "Tap sent us!"

Squinty eyes narrowed.

"We have a note." Soleil handed him the piece of paper.

Old Willy—who actually only appeared to be in his thirties—snatched the paper and read it over. He pushed open the door and an odd mixture of scents tickled my nose. "I owe Tap big time, so you're in luck. Come on in."

Soleil and I came inside. Old Willy slammed the door shut and slid five locks into place.

"Are you that worried about thieves?" Soleil asked.

"Yes," he said quickly. "I don't want anyone thinking I'm here. People have to respect my hours. Follow me upstairs."

He led us around shelves filled with bottles of every shape, size, and color until we reached a narrow, winding staircase. Each step creaked and moaned as we went up. Finally, we reached the top. It was a living area. It had a long table, a bed, a dresser, and a few shelves.

Old Willy motioned toward the table. "Have a seat. Do you

want some tea? I have some freshly brewed Assam Tonganagoan Estate—black, of course."

"Of course." Soleil smiled. "I'd love some, thank you."

"You?" Old Willy looked at me.

"Sure."

"Be right back." He disappeared down the stairs.

"What do you make of this?" I whispered.

Soleil shrugged. "If Tap trusts him, then so do I."

"I just hope he can help us."

"This guy could come in handy. I hate relying on witches, anyway. If Old Willy can do even some of what Gessilyn can, we're in luck."

"I guess you're right."

Old Willy returned, balancing three delicate tea cups. He set one in front of each of us and then sat down. "What do you two need? It's not every day I get a werewolf and a valkyrie walking in together. Sounds like the beginning of a bad joke, actually." He cracked a smile.

I didn't. "Look, Old Willy, we—"

"Oh, I'm not Old Willy. That's my dad. I'm Darrell." He held out a hand.

"Toby." I shook his hand.

"Soleil." She shook it, too.

"Tap says you can run locator spells," I said.

Darrell sipped his tea and nodded. "I can. I assume you have something belonging to the missing person."

My stomach sank. "Will a picture work?"

"You don't have anything else?"

"Not on me. I wasn't expecting her to go missing."

Darrell set his cup down. "Tell me one of you is related to

her."

Soleil and I shook our heads.

"Is she in love with either of you?"

"Me," I said.

"Okay, I can throw a love potion in the mix. That'll help. Tell me what you know about where she could be. Who she might be with." He sipped his tea again.

"Seattle," Soleil said. "We were out shopping with a vampire and some humans when another werewolf showed up. Victoria ran, and we haven't been able to find her."

"Might she be in danger?" Darrell continued sipping.

"That's why we're here," I said. "Her family pack is extremely dangerous, as is mine. If any of them get their hands on her—" Anger pulsated through me. "They'll regret ever returning from the other side."

Darrell nodded. "So, they came back from the other side with the mass exodus?"

"Even she did," Soleil said.

"That was the strangest thing I've ever seen," Darrell said. "Ain't never seen anything like that. So many supernatural creatures stepping out from a giant rip in the earth. Even creatures you thought were nothin' more than tales—they were real. The fog, too. More colors than a flipping rainbow. It shone like a—"

"Yeah, I was there, too. We need to find Victoria. Those wolves won't hesitate to kill her."

His eyes bulged. "Okay, let me gather my ingredients. Get her picture out and think all the lovey-dovey thoughts you can about her. The potion is going to draw from your feelings."

"What can I do?" Soleil asked.

"Help me gather what we need." Darrell rose from his seat. Soleil followed him down the stairs.

I pulled out my wallet and slid the old picture out of the plastic sleeve and put it on the table. My heart ached, looking at her beautiful face. "We'll find you," I promised her.

Downstairs, I could hear footsteps and shuffling around.

"Third shelf, bottom right," Darrell said. "Tall, blue container."

I took a deep breath and focused on the picture. The last thing I wanted was to be apart from her for a long time again. I wasn't sure I could take it. Sure, I'd managed during her death. I'd focused on bringing peace between werewolves and vampires. It had lasted until the mass exodus of the dead, as Darrell had put it. Now, there was nothing to show for all my efforts.

But as long as I had Victoria, none of that mattered. She was all I cared about—and she was gone again.

My heart constricted as I stared at the photo. It was fading, despite how well I'd tried to take care of it. I pulled out my phone and gave her number another call. That time, it went straight to voicemail. I sighed and went over to my pictures.

I scrolled through recent pictures. I'd taken so many, some of the pack teased me—not that I cared. I knew the value of having pictures of her. There was no way I could get enough of her beautiful, smiling face. She could light up a room at midnight with that grin.

The images scrolled by, and I stopped at one of the two us. A selfie I'd taken on my porch shortly after her memories of us had returned—not that it had been all that long yet.

My head snapped up. Darrell and Soleil were downstairs,

still hunting down ingredients. Glass clinked. Chairs rubbed against the wood floor. Soleil asked questions and Darrell answered.

My stomach grew tighter by the moment. It felt like we were using valuable time, but what other option did we have? Going to Seattle would be useless unless we knew exactly where she was.

I went back to my contacts and called her again.

Nothing.

"Where are you?" I whispered.

The stairs creaked and groaned as they made their way up. Soleil and Darrell both came up, their arms loaded with glass bottles. Darrell even balanced a couple bowls over the back of his head.

I arched a brow. "Do you need help?"

"Just focus on your love for the girl," Darrell grunted.

They set the bowls and jars on the table.

"I'm serious." Darrell frowned.

I turned my attention back to my phone.

"You better not be texting," he complained.

"I'm looking at our recent pictures together."

"Oh, I want to see," Soleil exclaimed.

"Focus," Darrell snapped. "You guys want to find her, and I want to get home."

"This isn't your home?" she asked.

From the corner of my eye, I watched him shove three bottles toward her. "Mix two teaspoons of the pink powder with an eighth of a cup of the green and six ounces of the red liquid." He turned to me, with beads of sweat forming around his hairline. "Focus on your love!"

I turned away from them and continued through the images of Victoria and me, trying to put everything else out of my mind—especially the fact that we didn't know where she was.

My heart warmed at a selfie of us snuggling in the living room, while watching a movie with the pack. That embrace had led to a series of sneaky kisses until Dillon noticed us. He and the pack had teased us until we took it out to the porch.

"Okay, we're ready." Darrell's voice broke my concentration.

I jumped and turned back to them.

"Ready?" He stirred a bubbling concoction. It smelled like tree bark and daisies.

"Sure. I suppose I have to drink that."

Darrell shook his head. "Nope. I have to smear it on your skin."

I gave him a double-take.

"You and her, both. She saw the girl last, and you love her. Roll up your sleeves."

Soleil and I exchanged a worried glance.

"You want to find her or not?" Darrell snapped.

I slid off my jacket and rolled my sleeves as far as they would go. Darrell continued stirring for a moment and then brought the bowl over to me. Without a word, he scooped some of the liquid in the spoon, and it slathered on my skin. It was startlingly cold and it yet it bubbled, even on my skin. Once that forearm was covered, he covered my other one.

Soleil touched the skin on her arm and arched a brow as she watched me.

Darrell put the spoon back and stirred again. He turned

back to me and put the concoction on my face.

I gasped in surprise.

"Hold still," he muttered, still smearing. Then he turned to Soleil and repeated the process.

"Don't get that on my shirt," she said.

"Quiet. This is an important part of the process." He turned to me. "Continue focusing on the loving feelings. Think about everything you love about her."

I closed my eyes and thought about our last kiss.

"Don't close your eyes yet!"

My eyes flew open. "I didn't mean to."

"Don't talk," he snapped.

I exchanged an annoyed glance with Soleil as Darrell smeared the gunk on her face. When he was done, he moved back to where he'd been sitting.

"Don't you have to wear that?" Soleil asked.

"I'm not connected to her." He stirred what was left in the bowl. "*Now* you guys can close your eyes. Just think about her—especially everything you can about your most recent interaction with her. Did you tell me her name?"

"Victoria," I said.

"Okay, just focus on Victoria. I'll do the rest." It sounded like he moved the bowl back and forth.

My thoughts returned to our last kiss. It had been more rushed than I would have liked, given that our nerves were on edge over the dead body and I was headed to the poker game.

Darrell whispered in a foreign language that I wasn't familiar with.

I wanted to focus on other times we'd spent together—times not rushed. We'd had some wonderful shared moments, appreciating being with each other, especially after her memories of me had returned.

Darrell's voice rose, and it became clear that he was speaking German.

I'd learned several languages over the years, but that hadn't been one of them. It was too bad, because I wanted to know what he said.

"Do either of you see anything?" Darrell asked.

"Like what?" Soleil asked.

"I'll take that as a no," he muttered. "Think as hard as you can about your most recent interactions with Victoria." He spoke in German again, this time, practically shouting.

It was hard to think about anything over the sound of his voice, but I managed to pull up some memories of Victoria. They were all old memories, from before her death. We'd run off for secret dates in the woods as often as possible. It had been extremely risky, given that we were both children of rival alphas.

"Got it!" Darrell shouted.

My eyes flew open. "What?"

Darrell stared into the bowl. "She's right there. Look."

Soleil was closer, and looked in. Her face paled.

My heart plummeted.

CHAPTER 12

Victoria

A BEEPING NOISE WOKE ME. I struggled to open my eyes. I was in a hospital room and the noise came from behind a curtain.

My friends rested in the chairs by a window, only Soleil was missing. Sasha, Jacey, and Cheyenne were all sleeping. Ziamara flipped through a magazine. She rarely ever slept—apparently, that was typical among vampires.

Zia glanced over at me, her eyes wide. "You're awake! How do you feel?"

"Sore, but otherwise okay."

She set the magazine down and scooted the chair closer to the bed. "What happened?"

"Long story. How did you know I was here?"

"The cop who found your purse called the emergency numbers you set. Toby didn't answer, so he called Sasha next."

"Toby didn't pick up? Is he okay?"

"Probably busy trying to figure out what's going on with the bod—" She cleared her throat. "You know."

"Yeah." I ached all over, so I closed my eyes. "Where's Soleil?"

"She went back to Moonhaven to find Toby."

"I want to talk to him." I opened my eyes again and tried to sit up. "Can I borrow your phone?"

"Sorry. Mine runs off unicorn horn flakes and faerie dust. I didn't bring extra, thinking we'd be home by now."

"What about one of their phones?" I glanced over at the other girls.

"You want to use one of their phones to call *Toby*?"

My heart sank. They only knew him as the professor. I couldn't even risk calling him while they slept, just in case they woke while I was on the phone. "Did the doctors say when I can leave?"

Ziamara frowned. "Not now. You're dehydrated." She glanced toward my IV. "They couldn't tell us much—privacy laws or something—but I read their minds to figure out that's their main concern. Everything else looks good."

"Can't you use your *other* powers to get me out of here?"

She arched a brow. "Which one, exactly."

I glanced around to make sure no nurses were around and mouthed, "Mind Control."

Ziamara shook her head. "You need to be hydrated." She scooted closer and whispered, "But I did use it to convince the nurse to let all of us sleep in here. She wanted all of us to rest in that noisy waiting room. I'd be fine, of course, but I couldn't do that to them."

"That was nice of you." I sighed. "This whole thing sucks. Franklin ruined everything." But at least I'd kicked him in the 'nads. Hopefully, it still hurt.

"Is that the guy you ran from?" Her expression softened.

"Yeah." I clenched my fists. "I hate him more than ever now."

"Who is he?"

A nurse came in. "Oh, good. Our patient is awake. How do you feel?"

I forced a smile. "Great. Really hydrated and energetic."

Ziamara shook her head.

The nurse chuckled. "Eager to leave?"

"You could say that."

"We'll see about that. I'm Maggie. Do you have any questions?"

"I just want to get home."

"Hopefully tomorrow. Let me check your vitals and talk to the doctor on duty tonight. It looks like you have plenty of people to take care of you when you're discharged."

"Yes, and they'll keep a close eye on me." I smiled again. "But like I said, I feel great."

She pulled out a thermometer and took my blood pressure and temperature. Then she stuck a thing on my finger that she said measured how much oxygen is in my blood. "We need to draw some blood to check your electrolytes since you've been getting IV fluids."

"Okay." I held out my arm and she drew the blood.

Ziamara's eyes turned red, and she turned away before Maggie could see. "I'm going to send this to the lab and consult with the doctor. I'll be back. Just push the red button if you need anything."

"Thanks." I waited for her to leave and turned back to Ziamara. "What was that?"

"What?" She picked at a nail.

"Your eyes. Why'd they turn red?"

"Shh!"

"Fine. Read my thoughts."

She held my gaze.

Why did your eyes turn red at my blood? Werewolf blood is poisonous to you.

Ziamara played with the nail again. "I've been building up a tolerance."

"You can do that?"

"Seems to be working."

"Has anyone done that before?" I asked.

She shrugged.

"You worried about the pack?"

"It's complicated."

"Tell me. I can keep a secret."

"Promise not to tell Toby?"

My heart raced. I didn't want to keep anything from him. "Why?"

"He'll be worried about me getting hurt."

"What?" I exclaimed.

"But I won't," she said quickly. "You know how he worries about the pack."

I nodded. "Tell me what's going on."

She leaned close and whispered in my ear. "I want to be able to drink Jet's blood. It's what vampires do with their mates. He's willing as long as it doesn't hurt me."

I stared at her. "Have you?"

"I'm up to about ten drops." She sighed. "It's still a long way from *drinking*, you know?"

"Right. But I thought the taste was gross to you guys."

Ziamara shrugged. "I got used to the scent living with the pack, and that was the first step. Also, love-saturated blood always tastes better—and he does love me." She grinned.

Sasha sat up. "Blood? Huh? Is something wrong with her blood?"

"Nobody said blood," Ziamara fibbed. "But Victoria's awake, and she feels better."

My roommate stretched. "Good. So, you're okay?"

"Never better." I paused. "Well, that's not true. I hate being here, but you know what I mean."

Sasha rubbed her eyes. "Why'd you run off like that? What happened?"

Ziamara arched a brow at me.

"There's this guy. He, uh… Well, he's kind of an ex. It's really complicated."

"Maybe you need a break from guys. You're still getting over Carter, aren't you?"

"We're friends."

"Right." Sasha snorted. "That always works so well after a breakup."

"We *are* friends."

"If you say so." She gave me a look that clearly said she didn't believe me.

I opened my mouth to defend myself, but quickly closed it.

Maggie returned. "Sorry, hon. The doctor wants to keep you for observation overnight. Can I get you anything to eat? It's too late for a meal to be brought up, but we have a kitchenette down the hall, and I can grab you something."

Disappointment washed through me. I just wanted to head back to Moonhaven. "No, thanks."

"The good news is your friends can stay the night here if you want."

"You don't restrict visiting hours?" I asked.

"Not unless you want to kick them out." She winked.

I shook my head, trying to think of another way out. Sneaking out was a possibility, but I was too tired.

"Holler if you need anything." Maggie left the room.

Sasha rose and stretched. "Want me to sneak you some pizza or something else better than hospital food?"

"Can you sneak me out?"

She shook her head. "If they want to keep you a little longer, I'm sure it's for a good reason."

"Are you a doctor now?" I asked.

"Ha, ha." She turned to Jacey and Cheyenne. "You guys hungry?"

Cheyenne muttered nonsense and rolled over to the other armrest. Jacey didn't budge.

Sasha turned to Ziamara. "You wanna come?"

Zia glanced at me. "You mind? I'm kinda hungry. We can bring you back some."

I shook my head. "I'm not hungry, but go ahead. You guys eat."

"You sure?" Sasha frowned.

"Yeah, go. I need some sleep, anyway."

She grabbed my hand and squeezed. "Okay. We won't be long. I promise."

"No worries. Maybe you'll meet a cute guy." I smiled.

Her face lit up. "Yeah. Let's go." She woke the others and they all hurried out of the room.

"Have fun." I closed my eyes, hoping I'd be able to get some more sleep. With all my aches and pains and the fact that I'd just woken up a little while ago, I didn't hold out much hope. The same beeping that woke me continued.

A voice from deep within told me to try, anyway. Now I recognized it as my inner wolf. It was the same voice that had shouted at me while I was dating Carter, but didn't know I belonged with Toby. I'd found it annoying at the time, but now I was grateful. I hadn't taken things too far with Carter, although I had still managed to hurt him.

I felt bad for him. He was a pawn to his own father, and I knew how that felt—to be nothing more than something to be used by the one who had given me life. Carter deserved to find someone who loved him as much Toby did me.

My muscles relaxed, and I moved to a state that felt halfway between being asleep and awake. Though aware of being at the hospital, I dreamed.

When I felt a kiss on my cheek, I thought it was a dream.

"Look at those bruises." That sounded like Toby's voice.

My eyes flew open. Toby and Soleil stood at the side of my bed. Was I still dreaming?

His expression softened and he took my hand. "Are you okay?"

I nodded, my vision blurring with tears.

"What happened?"

I swallowed. "Franklin."

Toby's eyes narrowed. "He did this to you?"

"He didn't walk away unscathed, either. I'll bet he's still walking funny."

"How did he find you?" Soleil asked, worry covering her face.

I rubbed my swollen eye. "They're living over here."

"And I let you go without any other wolves." Toby shook

his head. "Some pack leader I am. Some fiancé."

"You're the best." I squeezed his hand. "Don't blame your-self."

"Where is he now?" Toby demanded.

"I have no idea."

"Does he know you're still in town?"

I shrugged.

"You didn't tell him where we live?"

"Of course not."

"Good." He sat on the edge of the bed. "When are they letting you go?"

"In the morning. They just want to keep me for observa-tion."

He glanced around the small room. "Where's Ziamara?"

"She and the others went for something to eat."

"That means I can't stay long. It would be hard to explain why I'm here."

"You could say you were in the area and Soleil told you I was here. That she ran into you somewhere." I squeezed his hand harder. "Please don't leave."

He ran the back of his fingers along my cheek and stared into my eyes. "Trust me, Victoria. I don't ever want to let you out of my sight again."

"I'm not sure if that's sweet or creepy," Soleil said.

Toby shot her an annoyed expression.

She shrugged. "Well, at least you don't sneak into her room and watch her sleep. That would definitely be creepy."

Footsteps and female voices sounded in the hall.

Toby jumped up from the bed and stood next to Soleil.

The girls all came in. Shock covered Sasha's face. "Professor Foley?"

He nodded. "I ran into Soleil, and she told me Victoria was here."

"Wow, you're a dedicated teacher," Sasha said. "So, how are you? You know, after being missing."

Toby flinched. After rescuing him, I understood why. He'd been tortured by jaguar shifters, waiting to hand him over to his father who wanted to kill him personally.

"You look great." Soleil smiled.

"Is it true?" Sasha asked. "Were you abducted?"

He nodded. "But it's over now. I'm just glad to be back to home and work. Well, this room is pretty full. I'll get going." He turned to me. "I hope you feel better Victoria." He glanced at me with longing in his eyes. "I'll be in the waiting room," he whispered. "Bye, girls."

"Bye," we all replied.

I watched as he left the room, wishing he didn't have to, but we couldn't let anyone think we were together. Not if he was going to keep his job. There was no way anyone would understand—or believe—our past.

Sasha sighed. "It's so hard to believe someone that hot is a professor."

The corners of my mouth twitched. It was hard to disagree.

She yawned. "I'm going to try to get some sleep. You up to shopping tomorrow if they let you out early enough?"

I shuddered at the thought of running into anymore of my old pack. "I have to get back and work on my homework."

Ziamara gave me a knowing look. She probably wanted to get back to Jet, too.

CHAPTER 13

Victoria

I DROVE THROUGH THE GATE at Moonhaven and pressed the remote to close it behind me. It was already dark outside. Lights shone from inside the mansion, and as I parked next to the camouflage Hummer, I could see a small group still around the body.

Alex trotted over as I got out of the car. He nuzzled me, and I rubbed between his ears. "What's going on?"

He didn't reply, of course.

As much as I wanted to see Toby, I was curious what was going on. After Sasha fell asleep, Toby had come into my hospital room and filled me in on everything he'd learned, which wasn't much.

Alex stayed at my side as I made my way over to Gessilyn, Killian, and a handful of witches I didn't recognize.

Gessilyn turned to me, tightening her ponytail. She was covered with dirt and grass stains.

"How's it going?" I asked.

She sighed. "We've been running spell after spell, trying to figure that out. So far, all we know is that the body was cursed with black magic."

"That's what Toby told me when I was in the hospital."

Gessilyn gave me a double-take. "What?"

"My old pack found me in Seattle. I got into a bit of a scuffle, but I'm fine."

She stepped closer and studied my face. Gessilyn's fingers traced my tender bruises and then she held her palm over them and closed her eyes. "They're still looking for you—with renewed vigor now."

Dread washed through me, but did I really expect a different answer?

"You were engaged to one of them?" she asked.

I stood taller. "I'm engaged to Toby. He's the only one—ever."

She arched a brow.

"Fine. My father pledged me in marriage to Franklin long ago, but I never agreed to it. I was running from the wedding when I was murdered."

Gessilyn nodded. "It all makes sense."

Another pretty blonde turned to us. She pulled some straight hair behind her ears. "Who's this?"

Gessilyn put a hand on my shoulder. "This is Victoria."

The blonde's eyes widened and she smiled. "*You're* Victoria." She threw her arms around me.

I gave Gessilyn a confused look and then hugged my new friend.

"This is my sister, Frida," Gessilyn said. "My family played an important part in helping Toby to find you."

Frida stood back and smiled. "It's so nice to finally meet you. We can all relate to your family problems. We walked away from the coven we grew up in."

Another blonde, this one with curly hair, turned to us. She looked a lot like Gessilyn and Frida. "Victoria? So great to meet you." She threw her arms around me. "I'm Roska, the youngest of the family."

"It's a pleasure."

"Let me introduce you to the rest of my family," Gessilyn said. "Hey, you guys!" She introduced me to her parents and siblings, all of whom also engulfed me in warm embraces.

Johan, Gessilyn's father, raked his fingers through his hair. "I'm quite unfamiliar with the type of dark magic surrounding this body." He frowned. "It's clearly been cursed, but we can't read into what type of curse it is or whom it will affect."

"So, we could all be cursed because of it?" I asked.

"I can't rule that out, given all the strange things going on, but it could also be aimed at someone in particular. If it's been here a while, it could be for a former resident."

"That's what we all hope," Roska said. "You have a really special pack here. It feels more like a family than the coven I grew up in."

I smiled. "I think so, too. It's all Toby—he's done all the work. I can't wait to be part of it."

Gessilyn's brows came together. "What do you mean? You're every bit a part of it as anyone else."

"I still live at the Waldensian."

"Doesn't matter," Frida said. "You could live on the other side of the world, and you'd be in the center of everything here because Toby holds you in his heart."

My face flushed, and I glanced to the side. "Speaking of him, I should get inside and let him know I'm here. Do you guys need anything? Something to eat or drink?"

"Thanks," Nora said, "but Brick just filled us up. I don't think I could eat for another week."

I laughed. "I believe that."

They all returned to the body and I headed inside. The television blared from the living room, but I went to the kitchen, where I heard Toby's laughter.

He, Brick, Sal, Dillon, and Soleil sat at the table, eating crumb cake with a red sauce drizzled over the top. Brick and Soleil sat next to each other, their fingers interlaced.

Toby was in the middle of telling a story and hadn't noticed my arrival. I slid into the seat next to him and smiled as he shared about a run-in with a newly-turned vampire. Sal grinned at me, but no one else showed any indication that they saw me. Toby leaned over the table, his story growing more intense.

I grabbed a slice of the cake and took a bite. The warm, sweet taste of cherries exploded in my mouth.

Finally, Toby finished his story and sat back, his arm brushing my shoulder. He turned to me, his eyes wide with surprise. "How long have you been here?"

"Long enough to hear most of your story." I smiled sweetly.

He wrapped his arms around me and pulled me from the seat, spinning me around. "It's so good to have you back. Did you get your projects done?"

"Mostly. My stats professor is pretty mean, though."

"Oh yeah? I'll need to have a word with him." Toby pressed his lips on mine and devoured my mouth with sweeping strokes of his tongue. Breathless, I gave myself to the kiss and returned the passion with equal intensity.

Dillon cleared his throat. "I'm going to see what movie the others are watching."

Toby let go of me. "No, we'll take this elsewhere. I want some time alone with this beauty."

I giggled. He took my hand, and we ran out of Moonhaven.

"Where are we going?" I asked.

"Somewhere quiet." He led me toward the woods.

"Like old times." My heart warmed, remembering so many secret dates in the woods our old packs used to fight over.

"Exactly. Only this time, we aren't breaking any rules."

"Those old ways were ridiculous, anyway."

"I couldn't agree more." He stopped and pulled me close, gazing into my eyes. He ran his thumb over my knuckles. "Where are you keeping the ring?"

"Here." I pulled the necklace out from underneath my shirt. "I can't wait to show the world."

"Me, too. That's the only part of you being in my class that I don't like."

I pressed my lips against his. "At least I got assigned to your class. Otherwise, we may have never run into each other."

He shuddered. "Don't talk like that. Let's go into the woods. There's a brook I want you to see. It reminds me of the one we used to like."

My heart warmed. "All we need is a picnic."

He ran his fingertips along my jawline. "All I need is you," he said, his voice husky.

Chills ran down my back, and I shivered.

"Come on. It isn't too far away." He led me through the woods.

My mind raced, remembering all the times we'd sneak away in the other woods—and the memories were so fresh and crisp, as though I'd never had them stolen in the first place. There were a few that hadn't ended so well, but most were wonderfully sweet and romantic.

After a few minutes, I could hear the sounds of water bubbling. "We must be close."

"We are."

A lump formed in my throat and tears threatened. After everything we'd been through—so many against our relationship—we were finally safe together. He had officially proposed, and now it was only a matter of time before we could marry.

We darted between some thick trees and around scratchy bushes. The brook came into sight. It really was like the one Toby and I had spent so much time near so long ago. A picnic sat before us.

I turned to him, tears pooling in my eyes. "How…?"

He kissed my right eye and then my left. "I told Sal to run ahead and set it up as soon as you arrived."

"It's perfect," I whispered. A single tear ran down my cheek, stinging my still-bruised face.

Toby trailed kisses along the path of my tear. "I hope that's a tear of happiness."

I nodded, too overwhelmed to speak.

He put an arm around my shoulders and led me to the blanket and we sat. "I won't feel safe until our fathers are dead again, but this brings back so many memories. I can't tell you how many times I thought back to our many trips in the woods over the years while you were dead."

"I'm sure I thought about them, too."

Toby tilted his head. "What do you mean? Those memories haven't returned?"

"They were crystal clear when I crossed back over to the land of the living, but from the moment I actually stepped across the threshold, my memories from the other side grew fuzzier by the minute. I don't think that had anything to do with the jaguars."

"I've heard others with similar stories after crossing over. Apparently death just isn't that memorable." Toby ran his fingers through my hair and smiled, but I couldn't return the smile. He kissed me. "Let's talk about happier things—like being back together, alone, and engaged."

I nodded and returned the kiss. He pulled me closer, kissing me deeply. My body relaxed, knowing I was home because I was there with him. He ran his hands through my hair again and then down my back, sending a warm shiver through me. The water continued to bubble and forest critters ran around nearby.

It was the most romantic moment I'd ever experienced.

"I promise to keep you warm." Toby slid off my jacket and took hungry possession of my mouth.

My heart raced. I pressed myself against him and kissed him just as greedily.

He fell back against the blanket and pulled me with him. "Sometimes it's still hard to believe you're really back. You were gone so long..."

"And I'm not going anywhere, ever."

"Good." He nibbled on my ear. I gasped, enjoying the light tickle. Toby pressed kisses along my shoulder and followed the collar of my scoop neck around my back.

The sweet and alluring scent of his love and desire surrounded me, taking over all of my senses. It was one of the best parts of being a werewolf—the strong senses that allowed me such a precious intimacy.

Toby gasped.

"I like it, too," I whispered.

He sat up and pulled me up, also. His eyes were wide and his face pale. The aroma of his desire pulled away.

"What is it?" I looked behind me, fully expecting to see one of our fathers. It was just the peaceful brook. I turned back to him. "What happened?"

Toby went to my back and tugged down on my shirt's collar. "You have a mole back here."

"Okay?"

"It was never there before."

"Those things show up all the time on skin, right?" I asked.

He came back around and looked at me. "It's almost in the shape of a *J*."

My heart plummeted. Just like all those mysterious jaguar references after I'd lost my memories. That had to be it. "What does it mean?"

Toby pulled me close and kissed the top of my head. "I have no idea, but I don't think it's good."

"Could it be some kind of…" I searched for the right word. "A sign that they've somehow claimed me?"

He shook his head. "You were bait for me, remember?"

"But his father had no problem with Carter having an interest in me."

An expression of terror and then anger ran across his face.

"Someone said something about how jaguars are supposed to mate by a certain age—and that Carter's close."

"So, it might be a claim on me for Carter?" I felt sick to my stomach. "How many people think they own me?"

"Too many," he grumbled. "Nobody owns you—not your father, not Franklin, and most certainly not those jaguars. Let's add this to the list of things to explore while trying to figure out how to make you shift."

A thought struck me. "Wait. You don't think that mole has something to do with why I can't shift?"

CHAPTER 14

Toby

I STARED AT VICTORIA, A mixture of terror and anger pulsing through me. Fear for how long it would take for the full moon to kill her if she didn't shift soon and fury for the jaguars who had done this to her.

She trembled. "At least we know it's there now. It's a new clue."

"I'm going to kill them."

Victoria shook her head. "We just need to get to the bottom of this, then Gessilyn can fix it."

"And then I can fix *them*."

"Toby," she whispered.

I bit back more threats toward the vile jaguars and gazed into her beautiful, dark eyes. "Yes?"

She ran her fingers through my hair and moved closer to me. "Don't let them ruin our moment together. They, along with our fathers, have already stolen so much from us. Let us have this picnic, please."

My anger melted. I nodded. "You're right."

Victoria pressed her sweet lips upon mine. "Let's just enjoy our time alone. We have a busy week ahead of us, and I have a feeling I'll probably only see you in class—and I won't be able to do this then." She closed her eyes, pressed herself against me, and gave me a mind-melting kiss that made the woods spin around us.

I wrapped my arms around her and let everything else disappear. For the short time we had together, we were the only two people in the world. Nothing and no one else mattered. We were finally together after far too many years apart.

Things grew a little too heavy, so I backed away, gasping for air. "We should eat before the food gets cold."

She stared at me and pulled hair from her eyes. "Right. We want our wedding night to be special, so we should back off a bit, even though I would love nothing better than to kiss you all night long."

I sucked in a deep breath and nodded. "We need to start planning that ceremony. Soon."

Victoria smiled. "I couldn't agree more. Do you have anything in mind?"

"As long as we end up married, I'm not concerned about the details. Whether it's big or small, fancy or simple—all that's up to you, my sweetness. I want to give you the wedding of your dreams."

"Aw, you're so sweet. Honestly, as long as you're there, nothing else matters."

My heart warmed. It was hard to pull my gaze from her, but I managed. Together, we set up the picnic. Sal had put together some fruit salad, wine, candles, and dessert. It was perfect.

Victoria pulled out the candles and lit them while I poured

the drinks. She leaned against me as we faced the brook and ate the salad, followed by the pie. We sipped wine and stole kisses between eating.

The moon grew higher in the sky.

"We should get back so you can get some sleep. Finals are no time to be short on rest."

She turned to me and stole a kiss. "Except when I can spend time with a sexy professor."

"I hope I'm the only sexy professor you're spending time with." The corners of my mouth twitched.

"You'd better believe it." She kissed me again, a deeper, more passionate kiss.

As much as I wanted to continue our time together, I backed away. "I'm serious about getting you back. When you wake up tired, you're going to blame me."

"Happily. I'll remember this picnic and have no regrets." She moved to kiss me, but I ducked away. "You're such a tease."

I laughed. "And you're making it hard to stay single."

"We need to set a date."

"That we do. Why don't we plan on discussing all this during Christmas break? We can plan while decorating Moonhaven."

"Won't we decorate over Thanksgiving? That's coming up."

"You're right. It's right around the time of the full moon, isn't it?"

"I think so."

"Maybe you'll be able to shift by then."

Her eyes lit up. "I hope so. I really don't know if I can take another full moon without shifting." She shuddered.

I remembered the mark, and ran my finger over it. "We need to show that to Gessilyn before you go home."

She nodded, but then her face fell. "With her being so busy with the dead body, is she going to have any time to look into this?"

"Her entire family is on that case. One of them can pull away to help us."

Victoria sighed. "But if the entire pack is affected by the body's curse, that needs to be the priority. I'm sure I can make it through one more full moon. I'll take some pain pills before it has a chance to hurt."

I shook my head. "We can't risk the next un-shift killing you. They keep getting worse and your wolf needs to come out."

"I'm tough."

I frowned. "Nobody's *that* tough, sweetness."

"I'll tell you what." She took my hand and stared into my eyes. "When I see Carter in class tomorrow, I'll find out if he's learned anything new. Surely, he has to know something else by now."

"You really think he can find out?"

"His father doesn't know he's working with us. It's perfect."

"Just be careful. Please."

"I will."

"Don't forget he has feelings for you," I said.

"I know, but both of us know I only have eyes for you." She kissed my cheek.

"Well, go easy on the poor guy. I'd hate to be in his shoes."

She smiled. "You never will be."

My heart warmed, and the heat spread throughout my body. I pulled her close again and kissed her. "I hope I never lose my gratitude for having you back. Sometimes it seems so unreal—like I expect to wake up any moment."

Her face formed a slow frown. "Is that what happened? You'd dream of me, and then wake to realize I was dead?"

I ran my thumb over her knuckles and nodded. "It was the worst feeling in the world, and the disappointment never grew more bearable. It always hit me like a ton of bricks."

"Oh, Toby…"

"But you're here now." I cleared my throat. "That's all that matters. You're actually here." I held her close again and ran my palms over her hair, overwhelmed with the reality of having her with me. After a minute, I pulled back.

She laced her fingers through mine and squeezed my hand. "I'm sorry I did that to you—not that I'll ever regret saving your life."

"What did I ever do to deserve you?"

Victoria gazed into my eyes. "You don't know? For starters, you always loved me for me. You never expected anything from me that I didn't want—you know, you've respected my wishes. You've always believed in me—you've had an unflinching belief in me. In my old pack, it was always about what I could do for them. Especially for my father and Franklin, and obviously, they still think they own me. You've never thought that. You appreciate me."

"How could I not? You're the most beautiful and amazing person I've ever met." I cupped her face. "You're intelligent, gifted, caring, and so much more. To trap you in a cage—

actually or metaphorically—would be wrong. You deserve freedom, and I always want you to have that."

We gazed into each other's eyes without saying anything for a moment. I ran my fingers through her hair again, and as my hand went down her back, my finger grazed her new mole.

"We need to get back to Moonhaven," I said. "Gessilyn needs to see that."

She threw herself against me and squeezed me. "I love you."

"And I love you. More than you'll ever know."

"Can't we just leave school behind and run away together?"

"I think we're better off with the pack and our other friends—Gessilyn, Tap, and even Soleil."

"Yeah, you're right." She sighed. "I just don't want to go back to the Waldensian."

"I want you at Moonhaven, too. But you also deserve the college experience. There's nothing like it. In fact, you probably shouldn't spend so much time with your old, boring professor."

The corners of her mouth twitched. "I happen to like my old, boring professor. But if you're old, what does that make me?"

"Beautiful."

She laughed and then pulled back. "We should clean up the picnic."

"As much as I'd love to stay here forever, you're right."

We put everything inside the basket and then I carried it, and we headed on our way back with my other arm wrapped around her. She leaned her head against me. We walked quietly, enjoying each other and the soft sounds of the woods around us.

When we reached Moonhaven, Gessilyn and her family were still crowded around the grave. They were flipping feverishly through books and scrolls. Most of them had dark bands under bloodshot eyes.

"Why don't you guys come inside and get some sleep?" I asked. "We have plenty of spare rooms. Take your pick."

Nora glanced up and gave me an appreciative glance. "Thanks, Toby, but Johan has blessed us all with an anti-sleeping spell."

"Tell me you've at least made some progress."

Johan put an arm around Nora and nodded. "We've narrowed the curse down to having been placed in the last five years."

I let go of Victoria, stood next to the witches, and studied the body. "But with the decomposition, it looks like it's been there much longer."

Nora shrugged. "The curse could've caused that, or even the elements. Either way, I wouldn't try to figure out how long it's been there based on decay."

"That's true. Well, if you change your minds about sleep, come inside. We hardly use the third and fourth floors if you'd like privacy."

"Thanks, Toby." Nora smiled and then turned back to the body.

"We do have one more question for you," I said.

Gessilyn snapped her attention toward us. "What's the matter? Your tone worries me."

Apparently I couldn't hide my fear when it came to Victoria. "Can you take a look at this?"

Victoria turned around and pulled her hair in front of her shoulder. I pulled her collar away from the mole.

Gessilyn gasped.

"Jaguars?" Johan asked.

"It's the only thing that makes sense." I frowned.

Frida came over and ran a finger over the J-shaped mole. "Could this have something to do with why she won't shift?"

"I was hoping you'd know," I said.

Nora and Johan moved closer, studying it. Johan also ran a finger along it. "I've heard of using jewelry or spells to avoid the natural consequences of being a certain species, but a mole? Never." He turned to Nora. "Have you?"

She shook her head. "It's new to me, also. But then again, the jaguars seem to have brought in all kinds of new things. One of us is going to need to see if we can read the magic associated with it."

"I'll do it," Gessilyn said. "I'm frustrated with this body, anyway. I need a break."

"Let me know if you need any help," Frida said.

"We'll all help," Keran assured us.

I nodded a thanks, and then Gessilyn, Victoria, and I went inside the house. Sounds from the TV came from the living room.

"Let's go into my office." I led the way and closed the door behind us.

Gessilyn put her hand over the mole and closed her eyes. "I can feel magic." She held perfectly still. "It seems to be blocking something. Maybe we've found the source of the problem."

Victoria spun around, her eyes huge. "You can make me shift again?"

"Not this very moment, but if I can crack the spell, you may very well be able to run around with the pack at the next full moon."

I wrapped my arms around Victoria and glanced at Gessilyn. "How soon can you crack the code?"

"That's the big question. I don't recognize the magic. We're going to need to talk to your jaguar friend."

CHAPTER 15

Victoria

"WHAT ARE YOU GOING TO ask him?" Soleil asked as we walked into Massaro's classroom.

"I'm just going to tell him what we found." I shrugged and sat in my usual seat. Carter wasn't there yet.

Soleil glanced around. "Even with everyone around?"

"I'll watch how I word it."

"Did Toby give you any ideas this morning?"

"In class?" I held in a laugh. "Right. With all the girls clamoring for his attention, pretending not to get statistics."

"Was that where he was during lunch? Signing autographs?"

"Probably. No, he's busy with student appointments now. He says he's always extra busy between midterms and finals."

"Sucks for you."

"We have most of the month off between Thanksgiving and New Year. But with Toby busy, it gives me more time to get homework done. I barely got anything done last weekend. I can't wait for finals to be over."

"I'm sure being in Seattle had nothing to do with that."

"Nor did having a picnic in the woods."

"Speaking of that." Soleil raised an eyebrow. "How exactly did he find that J-shaped mark? Details. Spill 'em."

My face burned.

She laughed. "You're so easy to embarrass. Anyway, I wasn't kidding. Tell Soleil everything."

Massaro came in, saving me. For once, the man was actually sparing me from misery.

Soleil leaned closer. "Where's Carter?"

"Good question." I watched the door as Massaro set up his things on his desk. Carter always arrived early for class.

"Time for another quiz," Massaro said. "Open your devices and go to this webpage." He scribbled a URL on the whiteboard.

Several around me groaned. I wasn't much happier, having been focused on everything other than a psychology quiz over the weekend.

I took the quiz, continuing to watch the door from the corner of my eye. Carter was nowhere to be seen. Something had to be wrong.

"Submit your responses," Massaro said. "Then open your textbooks to page three-hundred-fifty-seven."

I had a hard time focusing on the lecture. With each passing moment, the sinking feeling in the pit of my stomach deepened. Carter was one of the most responsible students I knew.

What if his father had caught him spying for us? If he was in the torture room I'd found Toby in, I had no way of getting to him. My stomach twisted in knots.

Hopefully, I was overreacting. But after what I'd seen with my own eyes—Toby's mistreatment—I wouldn't put anything past Carter's dad. Especially since Carter was now helping us.

"Miss Bernhardt," Massaro boomed.

I jumped and stared at him.

"What's the answer?" He folded his arms and his brows came together like a fuzzy unibrow.

"Pavlov's dogs," Soleil whispered.

I swallowed, not looking away from Massaro. "P-Pavlov's dogs?"

"Is that a question?" he demanded.

"No." I hated how he could drive fear into me with a simple glance.

"Correct. It's all about classical conditioning." He turned around and spoke about ringing bells and saliva.

Shaking, I slunk down in my chair.

"You're welcome," Soleil whispered.

"Thanks." I pulled myself up and sat straight. Somehow, I managed to focus on what Massaro said through the rest of class, despite worrying about Carter.

As soon as the class ended, I texted him.

"Do you think something's wrong?" Soleil asked.

"How couldn't it be? His dad is a psychopath. He's the one behind my memory loss and the one who kidnapped and tortured Toby."

"You know, I wouldn't say that so loud."

I sighed. "Nobody else around here calls him Toby. Anyway, now Carter, who's supposed to run all the super-secret Jag stuff is working to help us."

"Maybe he's just sick. Did you think about that? There's a stomach virus going around."

"He'd have told me." I checked my phone. No new text.

"Something's wrong."

"I'm sure he's fine. Besides, we can't worry about him right now. We have your curse as well as that dead body to worry about."

"He's my friend," I snapped. "His life could be in danger. I can't not worry about him."

"Okay, let's just make sure he's in trouble before we jump to conclusions. Let's head over to Moonhaven."

"Sure. No, wait. You're going to have to go without me. I have a ton of studying. I hope I can concentrate when Carter might be in danger." Oh, how I wished I could do something to help him, but what? It wasn't like I could sneak into the Jag.

"How about we compromise? Let's head over to the Faeble. You study, and I'll see what Tap thinks. He probably knows a guy who knows a guy. You know?"

"Okay, fine. As long as I can study."

"This time of day? Of course."

I drove us to the Waldensian, parked, and we ran through the woods to the Faeble. Sometimes I really wished Tap had a parking lot, even though that went completely against every reasoning he had for the hidden bar.

Inside, it was pretty quiet. Some peppy music played from the speakers and the conversation was at a dull level. I wouldn't need a private room unless some rowdy creatures came in.

I waved to Tap and then sat at a table in the back. I made myself comfortable and spread out my stuff. With psychology fresh on my mind, I started with the latest project Massaro had thrown our way. I angled myself so I couldn't see Soleil deep in conversation with Tap. Otherwise, I'd be too tempted to focus on them.

After about an hour, I sent Carter another text. He had to have gotten too close to some powerful information and pissed off his dad.

My stomach lurched.

"Come on over here," Soleil called.

I needed a break, anyway, so I crammed my psychology stuff into my bag and hung it on the chair.

"Still can't get ahold of the jaguar?" Soleil asked.

"No." I slunk onto a barstool.

Tap gave me a sympathetic expression. "You can't get into the club?"

I shook my head. "Not without putting my life at risk. They're the ones who stole my memories and tortured Toby!" I clenched my fists.

"What about you?" Tap turned to Soleil.

"Nope. I'm on their naughty list, too."

Tap rubbed his chin. "There has to be a way to find out what's going on in there."

"You've got to know someone, big guy." Soleil leaned her chin against her palm and studied him.

"Not many are eager to go against the jaguars. They're rich, powerful, and mostly unknown—and that's the scariest part."

"No ideas?" Soleil sipped her rainbow drink.

I covered my face with my hands.

"I'll have to get back to you. You want something to drink?" Tap asked.

Something hard sounded great—so I could forget about all our problems—but I had studying to do. "Maybe something light. I have so much studying left."

Tap spun around and mixed together liquids from various bottles into one tall, skinny glass. He brought it over, filled with an orange-red drink. "This ought to be just perfect."

"Thanks." I took it and downed it in one swig. It tasted like cranberries and grapefruit.

"I thought you'd sip it while studying," Tap said. "But that works, too."

I laughed bitterly. "I'd better get back to my studies."

"Are you going to keep up with your classes after the quarter ends?" He tilted his head.

"Toby wants me to."

"What do you want?"

I shrugged. "I guess it depends on how all this plays out. From the sounds of it, if I don't shift soon, I might not be able to do much of anything."

Tap and Soleil both grimaced. Then Tap's eyes widened and he turned to Soleil. "Why don't you drink her essence?"

"Again?" I asked.

"You have all your memories restored, right?" Tap asked. "The love's kiss spell worked, didn't it?"

I nodded and glanced between the two of them. "You think she might figure out something about where Carter is? Using my memories?"

"It's possible," Tap said. "That's all I'm saying. What do you have to lose?"

"My essence. Do I have an endless supply of that stuff?"

"It rebuilds after a while," Soleil said. "You're fine."

I wasn't so sure. "I'm not going to run out if you keep doing that, am I?"

"You—"

"It's not going to shorten my lifespan is it?"

"I'm telling you—"

"How do you know the essence rebuilds? What if it doesn't?"

She shook her head. "If you don't want me to try to help with Carter, I won't."

I frowned. "It's not like I know anything about essence. They don't exactly teach it at school."

"They do in Valhalla." She arched a brow.

"Really?"

"Yes. I assure you, it continues growing and replenishing itself. I'm hardly the only way it diminishes."

"What do you mean?" I asked.

"It dwindles after a really bad scare or an injury, for example. Many things can do it. Then it starts rebuilding. It's very flexible—as it should be since its entire purpose is to keep people going. People say the body can do miraculous things. What do you think helps it to keep going?"

"Essence," I said.

She nodded. "It's most versatile, but I won't take any more if you don't want me to." She finished her drink. "I hope Carter's okay."

I knew what she was doing, but I couldn't say no. "Okay. Let's do this. See if there's anything in there about my ability to shift. Maybe there's something I haven't put together about the mole."

Soleil rubbed her hands together. "Let me have a look-see."

I closed my eyes, beginning to feel like a pro at the whole essence-drinking thing. It had been done to me enough times by now. My body relaxed, and my mind did, as well. Time seemed to stand still as my essence left my body.

"You should stop," Tap said in the distance.

Soleil continued.

My body was so relaxed, it nearly went limp.

"Soleil!" Tap called.

A scuffle sounded somewhere.

Her wings caused a breeze to blow my hair, my essence returned to me, and I fell back. My eyes flew open and I caught myself by grabbing onto the bar.

"What was that?" I asked.

"That's what I want to know." Tap now stood on our side of the bar, glaring at Soleil.

She leaned against the bar, her eyes dazed.

"What happened, Soleil?" I asked.

"That... it was..." She blinked a few times and turned her attention toward me. "You're not going to believe what I saw."

CHAPTER 16

Toby

I CLOSED MY OFFICE DOOR and leaned against it, exhausted. My last student appointment for the day had just ended. It had been a brutal afternoon—one appointment after another. Each person more confused than the last about something on the upcoming exam. If I didn't know better, I'd have thought some of them hadn't paid a bit of attention all session.

Part of me wanted to recline in my chair and sleep, but there was too much to do. I needed to find out if Victoria had spoken with Carter or if Gessilyn had figured anything out about either Victoria's new mark or the cursed body still on my property.

We really needed to get rid of that thing. What if the police were looking for it? I hadn't heard about any missing persons, but that didn't mean there weren't any, and people already had some crazy rumors going around about Moonhaven.

I yawned and ignored my aching muscles. It was funny how mental exhaustion was almost worse than physical exertion. Confused college students put more strain on me than fighting enormous, powerful supernatural creatures. I laughed at the thought.

My stomach rumbled, reminding me that I hadn't eaten since breakfast. I wanted to see Victoria, but she was probably bogged down with her own studies. I didn't want to pull her away from them. I'd just eat at home with the pack. Then I'd call her later if she didn't call me first. I didn't want to be the one responsible for her not getting her studies done.

Bleary-eyed, I collected my things and headed out of my office. Roger and some of the other math professors were gathered together.

I nodded toward them and headed for the stairs.

"Hey, Foley," Roger called.

"Yeah?" I stopped and turned toward the group.

"Great game on Friday. Still on for this week, right?"

My exhaustion squeezed me. I smiled. "Of course. Can't wait."

Fred elbowed an electrical engineering professor. "Foley's an animal."

"Funny." I shook my head. "Have a good night, guys."

"You, too," they all said.

My stomach growled again as I made my way outside into the dark night. I was sure glad that Brick enjoyed cooking. He'd been making my meals for so long—most of the time Victoria had been dead.

When I opened the front door of the mansion, an array of delicious scents greeted me—pot roast, spiced vegetables, creamy sauces, fresh bread, and some type of chicken. My mouth watered.

I threw my bag into my office and hurried into the kitchen. The table was full. Not a seat remained open for me. My entire pack was there along with Gessilyn and her family. I hadn't even noticed no one had been gathered around the makeshift grave.

Everyone greeted me.

Brick got up. "Sit down, sir."

"I don't want to take your seat."

"We're about to have some dessert, I need to prepare the sauce to drizzle over it."

"If you're sure."

"I am. Are you okay?"

"Just tired. Can't wait for these finals to be over." I grabbed a plate and silverware and took his seat.

"When are finals?" Dillon asked.

I groaned. "Please, I just want to eat my dinner and forget about them for a while." I filled my plate and then glanced toward the witches. "How are you all doing?"

"I think we may have cracked the curse," Gessilyn said.

"Oh?" I bit into the pot roast. It melted in my mouth. "Tell me everything."

"It appears to be from Central America," Frida said.

"That's where the jaguars originated."

She nodded. "I recognized part of the magic from some time I spent there, dating this guy who…" She glanced at her father. "Never mind. The point is, the curse is definitely from that region."

"What guy?" Johan asked. "When did you go there?"

Frida jumped up from the chair. "You need help with that, Brick? I've got you covered." She ran over to the stove.

Johan shook his head. "My children and their secret rune travels."

"I know all about that," Dillon muttered.

Gessilyn's face turned beet red.

Killian arched a brow. "Did I miss something?"

Dillon muttered something under his breath.

"We moved the rune," Gessilyn said.

Jet laughed. "I wish I could've seen that!"

"Really?" Dillon asked. "You want to see my—?"

"Gross!" Jet shoved Dillon. "No, I'd have loved to have seen her pop out of the mirror while you were in the middle of your business."

Killian's eyes widened as he looked at Gessilyn. "You arrived while he was going to the bathroom?"

"One time. And I'm never putting another rune in a bathroom again." Her face turned even redder. "Ever."

Killian burst out laughing. "That's hilarious."

"I'm never going to hear the end of this." Gessilyn shook her head.

I laughed, glad to enjoy a little comic relief, brief as it probably would be.

Brick pulled out a crumbled pie from the oven. Frida stirred something in a pot, and together they drizzled it over the dessert.

I filled my plate again. "Did you learn anything else about the body's curse?"

"It seems to be working with another spell," Nora said. "That's what made it so hard for us to figure out in the first place—it relies heavily on something else—probably the mole."

"What?"

"That's our next question. We need to speak with that jaguar friend of Victoria's."

"Yes, we do," I agreed. "He seems to be the key to all our questions. Has anyone spoken with Victoria? I've been bogged down with work all day."

Brick turned around. "She and Soleil are at the Faeble, talking with Tap. Sounds like they might be coming here later."

"At least I know she's safe."

"Soleil has hardly left her side." Brick beamed.

Despite all the stress, I smiled, happy for my friend. All the years he'd spent at my side, he'd been as lonely as me. Now we both had love—I just needed to find a way to for my love to shift before something went terribly wrong.

Frida placed pieces of the pie on dessert plates and Brick passed them out. I quickly finished my food and then ate the delicious treat with everyone. Frida gave everyone some sweet wine to go with the pie.

By the time I finished, I felt like a new man. My aches, pains, and exhaustion were gone. Once again, I felt like I could take on the world. I just needed to hear from Victoria first.

"What are we going to do with the body now?" Jet asked.

"Eventually, we'll burn it," Keran said.

"Not yet?" Jet asked.

Gessilyn gave me a tired smile. "Killian and I are going to stay here. I feel like we're finally getting close."

Killian nodded. "And I keep thinking the body and the new mark are somehow related."

"It's the jaguars." I frowned.

"Yes, but it's the magic we have to figure out," Killian said. "We need to find out what that young jaguar knows."

"Or what he can find out," Nora said. "Johan and I are

going to stay here until we have answers, also."

"I can't thank you enough," I said. "If you ever need any-thing…"

"Just keep feeding us like this," Eldon said, "and I'll give you any help I can."

Everyone laughed.

Johan rose and stretched. "I'm going to get some shut-eye." He turned to me. "Wake me when Victoria gets here. I want to see if the mark interacts with the magic at all."

"Will do."

The witches all made their way upstairs. The pack helped with kitchen cleanup and then we all went our separate ways throughout the large home. I went to my office, full and ready to fall asleep—but not before I spoke with Victoria. Or graded my enormous stack of papers.

I slunk into my chair and pulled out my phone. No missed texts or calls. Hopefully that meant she was busy studying and not that anything was wrong. It was too bad we were both so busy preparing for finals that she couldn't come over. What I wouldn't give to have her crawl into my lap and watch the fire in the fireplace together.

I went to our earlier texting conversation and sent her a quick text to let her know I was thinking about her.

Toby: I <3 u

Victoria: I luv & miss u

Toby: Any chance of coming over 2nite?

Victoria: I wish. Lunch tomorrow?

Toby: It's a date

Victoria: Does that mean I can kiss u?

Toby: Ha. I wish.

Victoria: Me 2

Toby: News on DB. Sure u can't come over?

Victoria: News on jags, but no I can't

Toby: What'd u find?

Victoria: 2 much 2 text

Toby: Come over. We can do our work 2gether

Victoria: Hard to say no

Toby: Then don't

I smiled, hoping I'd convinced her. I felt partly bad, knowing how much she had to do, but between what we'd both found out, we may have learned something big.

Victoria: OK. S & I'll b over asap

Toby: Victory!

Victoria: Haha. Cu soon <3

I found a bunch of kissing emojis and sent them. She sent a bunch more.

Grinning like a fool, I leaned back in the chair and sighed. I loved having her back—it was like we were young again. Better, actually. We weren't stuck living under the thumbs of our respective fathers, scared for the day we might be caught and killed for our defiance.

I got up and added a log to the fire. Then I walked around the office and thought about what I needed to get done before she arrived. Once she arrived, we'd get no work done, despite our best efforts. I picked up my bag. It had ended up stuffed under my desk when I'd thrown it in.

It took a couple minutes to get everything set up, then I got to work. I reminded myself to take on a TA, who could handle grading papers. That was what upperclassmen were for, after all.

I went into my notes app and wrote myself a reminder in all caps. I had plenty of responsible students to choose from. It was a matter of finding one who needed an easy elective credit.

I'd only made it halfway through my first stack of papers when a knock sounded. My head snapped up toward the door.

Victoria stood there, smiling. She looked tired, but as gorgeous as ever. I scrambled out of my seat and wrapped my arms around her. "You have no idea how much I've missed you. I'm not scheduling any more lunch appointments—that's reserved for you."

She planted her soft, sweet lips on mine. "I'm not going to argue with that."

I pressed my mouth over hers. She tasted citrusy. "Good." I scooped her up and brought her over to the loveseat that faced the fireplace.

Victoria held my gaze and ran her fingers through my hair. "This is nice."

"I switched to a different conditioner."

"Not your hair." She laughed. "Being here with you."

I gave her a playful pout. "You don't like my hair?"

"You're impossible, you know that?"

"I do my best." I grinned.

She gave me a quick kiss. "What did you guys find out about the body?"

"You want to talk about that now?"

"I thought I came over to do homework and discuss what we found out."

I kissed her in front of her ear. "I wish we could sip wine and stare into each other's eyes all night."

"You're really hard to say no to, you know that?"

"I *am* impossibly adorable." I batted my eyelashes.

She burst into laughter.

"You don't think so?" I brought my hand to my heart. "I can't believe this."

Victoria kissed my nose. "I do think so. That's the problem. I'd rather spend all my time with you, but the full moon's coming, and I'm no closer to shifting."

My mouth curved down. "Oh, sweetness. I didn't mean to make light of that."

She ran her fingertip along my stubble. "I know. It's hard to think about anything else when you're around, but I hate thinking of going through another full moon unable to shift." She shuddered. "I know I'm going to take pain pills, but I can't shake the feeling it might not be enough."

I held her close. "We're going to get to the bottom of this. Since the witches are having such a hard time finding the answers, I say it's time we look for another way to get to the bottom of this."

She sat back, her beautiful eyes wide and full of hope.

"What did you learn about the jaguars?"

"Soleil discovered that they know the cure to my curse."

My heart skipped a beat. "What is it?"

"We have no idea, but at least we know we're on the right track."

CHAPTER 17

Victoria

WE GATHERED AROUND THE MOSTLY-DUG up grave, the wind whipping my hair around my face. Gessilyn handed me a hair band.

"Thanks." I pulled it back into a loose bun.

Johan came over beside me. "Just stand still until I say we're done."

I nodded. He reached one hand out over the body and aimed the other one at my back, near the mole. My skin warmed, though he was at least a foot away.

"Do you feel that?" he asked.

"Yes."

"The magic is interacting. Did you notice anything before when you were near the body?"

I shook my head.

"Maybe it needs something to activate it," Roska said to her father. "It could be you."

"No, I'm just a vessel. It's not me personally—it could be any of us witches."

My skin warmed more, feeling like a hot iron was moving closer to my back.

"What's going on?" Toby asked, his eyes wide.

"It's just heating up. I'm fine."

He shook his head. "Look at her."

The others turned to me. Gessilyn gasped.

"What?" I exclaimed.

"You're… you're…" She stepped back, stumbling.

"What?" I begged.

"Glowing," Toby whispered.

My mouth dropped. I glanced down at my hands. They weren't illuminated.

"Your face." Roska moved closer, running her fingertips along my hairline.

"We should take her inside," Toby said.

"No," Johan said. "This is the closest we've come to discovering anything."

Toby took my hand. "Do you hurt? Are you uncomfortable?"

I shook my head. The wind picked up, blowing soggy leaves against us. The area around my mole warmed even more. "I'm fine. Let's see what we can learn. I'll do anything to be able to shift again."

"That's what I'm afraid of," he mumbled. "If you get the least bit uncomfortable, say so."

"Okay."

My skin continued warming until it started to feel hot. I held my breath and glanced over at the body. Its skin had a slight glow—probably similar to what I looked like.

"Are you all right?" Toby asked.

I nodded, not trusting my voice.

"Maybe we should stop."

"No!" I exclaimed. If this was all I had to deal with in order to turn at the moon, I would take it.

"Do you feel that?" Johan asked.

I turned to him, but he was talking to his family. Nora nodded and put her hands out toward the body and me. Gessilyn and her siblings did the same.

The heat grew unbearable. I cried out and threw my head back.

"Stop!" Toby demanded.

"We almost have it," Keran said.

Toby grabbed me and pulled me toward the house. "I'm not going to let this continue."

"I want to shift."

"There has to be another way." He brought me inside and lay me on the loveseat in his office. "We'll figure something else out. Hopefully they were able to read enough into the magic."

"I'm going back out there." I tried to pull myself up, but my back hurt with each movement I made. It felt like the skin had been horribly sunburned.

"Let me look at the mark." He brushed my hair, which at some point had fallen out of the bun, out of the way and pulled on the collar of my shirt. He gasped. "Your back is bright red. If you go out there, you could cause permanent damage."

"Not to mention possibly killing me," I muttered.

"There are other options."

"Not if my mole is connected with the body out there." I ran for the doorway.

Toby grabbed my arm and spun me around. "I won't let you get hurt further. We're going to have to do something about your skin as it is. It looks burned."

I narrowed my eyes. "There are six witches here—one is the high witch over all. They can fix my skin."

He held onto me. "No."

"No?" I exclaimed. "You're telling me no?"

"We need to think rationally about this."

"Now I'm not being rational?"

He took a deep breath. "That's not what I said."

"Actually, it is." I squirmed to get out of his hold. "Let go of me."

"Your emotions are on overdrive right now. Carter's missing and—"

"They can help me. That's why you brought them, right?" I pulled out of his grasp and ran outside.

"Victoria!"

I ignored him and ran back to the field. Gessilyn's whole family was still gathered around the body. "I'm back."

They turned toward me.

"Did you get what you needed?" Toby asked. "Her skin is burned. I hope you have a spell for fixing that."

Johan turned to him. "Do you want us to focus on a cream or this mess? I'd think a cursed body and a werewolf who can't shift would be the priority."

"So is her overall health. I want to introduce her to Darrell."

I spun around. "Who's Darrell?"

"He runs a spice shop."

"I don't need tea!" Tears blurred my vision. I turned to Gessilyn. "Do you need my mark again?"

Toby stepped between us and narrowed his eyes at her. "If

you do that again, I'm sending you all back home."

"What?" I gasped. "You wouldn't."

"Oh, I will. We can get to the bottom of this one way or another." He glanced over at the body. "For all we know, burning it will break your curse."

I shook. "I can't believe you."

"If you think I'm being unreasonable, show them your back."

Tears spilled onto my cheeks. "Fine." I pulled my hair over my shoulder and turned my back toward Gessilyn.

Several of the witches gasped.

"We need to do something about that," Nora said. She looped her arm through mine and led me back into the mansion.

Behind us, I could hear Toby discussing the curse with the others.

"Why didn't you say anything about the burning?" Nora asked.

"It isn't that bad."

"I beg to differ." She led me into the main bathroom and dug around the medicine cabinet. "Nothing I can use here. I didn't bring anything, either. Are you up for a quick trip?"

"What do you mean?"

"We'll travel by runes. Toby won't even know you've gone anywhere."

"It'll make my back stop hurting?" The pain was growing by the moment.

"Not the rune travel, but I know a lake whose mud will cure any skin ailment, even burns."

"Let's do it."

She took my hand and led me to an antique full-length mirror in the front room. "Close your eyes and don't open them until I say to."

I nodded and then closed my eyes.

Nora spoke in a foreign language. I felt a tugging sensation. It was hard not to open my eyes, but I managed to keep them closed.

"Open them."

I opened my eyes. We stood in a bathroom I'd never seen before. It was painted in brownish-orange tones and decorations that seemed like it was from a time long gone, yet the sink, shower, and toilet all seemed modern. "Where are we?"

"It's hard to explain, and chances are, you've never heard of it. Let me grab a jar so we can bring some of the mud with us." She opened the cabinet under the sink and pulled out a fat jar. "This ought to do it. Let's hurry, before Toby realizes we've left."

She led me through a dimly lit home.

"Is this your house?"

"Not so loud," she whispered. "And no, it's not. It used to be my mirror, though."

"Wait—what?"

"No time for questions." She pulled me along until we came to the front door. We ran down a sidewalk for a couple blocks until we reached some woods.

"Now can I ask where we are?"

"Yeah, but we need to hurry." She darted off the path and I struggled to keep up because of how much my back burned with every step. "I built a rune for traveling into that mirror. Though my old home was destroyed long ago, many of my things were salvaged, including several mirrors marked with runes. Wherever the mirrors are, I can go."

"Gessilyn, too?" I asked.

"Anyone with the magic of rune travel."

"Hold on. Are you saying *any* witch can use that portal in Moonhaven?" That left Toby and the entire pack in a vulnerable position.

"Definitely not." Nora ducked under a low-hanging branch. "Another witch would have either had to have been to Moonhaven first or brought in by someone who can use that particular rune—and that would only be us. Rune travel is one of those lost arts. Most witches today have never used it, much less know where to go to learn the craft."

Relief washed through me. "So, the pack is safe? No unwanted witches can get through."

She didn't respond.

"Nora?"

We rounded a corner and stopped in front of a lake.

"The pack is safe, right?" I repeated.

"It's more complicated than I explained to you—it would take months to get into all the nitty-gritty details. Rest assured we've placed protection blessings on the runes, making it hard for anyone with ill will to get through. For now, I need you to take your shirt off."

"Right here?"

She unscrewed the top off the jar. "Yes."

For as many times as I'd stripped in other woods to shift into my wolf form, I shouldn't have been surprised by the request. I was so out of habit, it felt odd. I was also used to having a pack around me and a full moon. The almost three-quarters moon that night reminded me I didn't have a lot of time left before I needed to be able to shift.

While she scooped mud into the jar, I pulled off my shirt slowly. Every time part of the fabric touched my skin, it felt like a jolt of electricity. Tears stung my eyes each time.

"My bra, too?" I cringed. Just the thought of touching it hurt.

"It might get muddy if you leave it on." She pressed the mud down, making room for more in the jar.

"I don't care about it that much."

Nora twisted the lid onto the jar, set it on the ground, and scooped some more into her palms. "Turn around."

I squeezed the shirt in my hands and turned my back to her. The cold, slimy mud felt good on my sore, hot skin.

"Looks like it's all covered. Let's head back. Toby's going to get suspicious soon."

We made our way out of the woods. A bright streetlight shone down on the sidewalk. I slid my shirt on, knowing it would probably end up ruined. We hurried back to the house with the rune.

"I hope whoever lives here didn't wake up and lock the front door," I said.

"Don't think like that." Nora turned the knob, and the door opened easily. We stepped inside, locked it, and made our way back to the bathroom. She handed me the jar. "Hold this and close your eyes."

Footsteps sounded in the hallway.

My eyes widened.

"Close them!" Nora whispered.

The footsteps grew closer.

I forced my eyes closed. My heart thundered, threatening to break through my ribcage.

Nora grabbed my free hand and squeezed, speaking in the foreign language again.

The bathroom door creaked as it opened.

I opened my eyes. We were back in Toby's front room. Relief swept through me and my knees buckled. I stumbled, but Nora grabbed onto me, helping me steady myself.

"We're back," Nora called.

"There they are," Dillon said from another room.

Toby, Brick, and a few others from the pack ran into the room. Relief flooded Toby's face and he ran over to me, kissing me all over my face. "What happened?"

"I had to get creative to find a salve for her burn," Nora said. "How's it working?"

"It feels better already." I reached around and patted the dried mud on my skin. It didn't hurt in the least.

He wrapped his arms around me, careful to avoid the burned areas. "I was so worried."

Gessilyn came in and smiled. "I told you she was in good hands with my mother."

Toby kissed my forehead. "Let's get you home. We've kept you from your studies long enough."

"Be sure to apply the mud until the jar is empty," Nora said.

I smiled and nodded, but my stomach twisted. With everything that I already had to worry about, applying a salve almost felt like too much.

What else could go wrong?

CHAPTER 18

Toby

THE NEXT WEEK AND A half went by in a blur of student meetings, classes, and faculty meetings while the witches pored over scrolls and books to find anything about the body's curse. I barely got to spend any time with Victoria—most days, I only saw her in class and at lunch. Beyond that, we had a few phone and text conversations, but nothing more.

Now that the exams were over at last, I was finally able to relax. I locked my office and went through the quiet building. A lot of the staff had already left for the long weekend. Everyone was eager for Thanksgiving, and then it would be time to go over the final projects and tests and enter in all my students' final grades.

The following week would be busy, despite most of the students being gone until the new year. Then I would have to think about preparing for the following quarter's classes. At least Victoria wasn't going anywhere—we just needed to get her to shift.

My throat closed up at the thought. Her burns had healed, but we were still no closer to finding her cure.

The full moon would come that night.

I pulled out my phone and sent Gessilyn a text.

Toby: *Anything?*
Gessilyn: *No. Sry.*
Toby: *We have 2 do something.*
Gessilyn: *Burn it.*

The body.

Toby: *U sure u got everything from it?*
Gessilyn: *Yes*

I frowned. Once we burned the body, there was no going back. If it didn't get rid of the curse, we would no longer have the source.

Toby: *Let's talk when I get home.*
Gessilyn: *OK*

At least that gave me a little time to mull things over. I climbed into my Hummer and turned it on, letting the engine warm. Victoria still hadn't found Carter, so there was no way of finding her cure from the jaguars without sneaking in—and after what I'd gone through, there was no way I would let anyone do that.

If I sent anyone in, I was basically signing their death warrant.

It was looking more and more like our only option was to bring in the vampires, as much as most of the pack didn't want to do.

My phone rang. It was the ringtone for Victoria's number.

I accepted the call immediately. "Hi, sweetness. Are you—

?"

"Toby." She sounded like she was crying.

"What's wrong?" I exclaimed.

"Everything."

"Where are you?"

"At the Waldensian."

"I'm coming over." I shifted into reverse and squealed out of the parking spot.

"You can't."

"Says who? You're upset." I pulled out of the lot and into traffic. It was unusually busy.

"You know why you can't come over."

"Then you'd better tell me what's wrong because I'm already on my way."

"I just found out I can't come back next quarter." Victoria sniffled. "My funds for my room and board have been cut. Sasha's already been assigned a new roommate from the waiting list. I have to pack everything up and move tonight. I shouldn't be surprised. I'm not under the jaguars' control anymore, and this was the last thing they were paying for."

"You seriously have that little notice?" I exploded. But why would that surprise us? The jaguars had probably planned that, too.

The light turned red and I slammed on the brakes.

"The new girl is moving in tomorrow."

"On Thanksgiving?"

"She's from Canada and not going home for our holiday. She's ready to move. Everyone wants to live in the Waldensian."

I ran my hands through my hair and yanked on the ends.

"It's the full moon!"

"Explain that to the head of campus housing."

"We'll set you up with a room at Moonhaven. You won't have to deal with a roommate. Plus, we'll be able to see each other whenever we want. Maybe this is for the best. But I'm coming over."

"No. Soleil's here. She's packing right now. Sasha's going to be so upset when she gets back."

My mind spun. "Can you two get everything packed before I shift?"

"I think so."

"You *think*?"

"Yeah. I just don't—ow!" Shuffling noises sounded.

"Victoria!"

"Are you there, Toby?" asked Soleil.

"What's going on?"

"She's been complaining about her bones aching. Looks like the shift is starting."

I swore. "She *can't* shift."

"Yeah, I know. Look, I'm going to get her on the bed. You're going to have to help me pack this stuff up. Stick on a hat and sunglasses so nobody recognizes you."

"I'll be right there."

Just before I ended the call, I could hear Victoria whimpering in the background.

When I pulled into the Waldensian parking lot, I parked in the back behind some trees. Then I climbed into the backseat, searching for a hat. I thought I had one somewhere. The back was filled with enough stuff for an impromptu camping trip.

By the time I stepped outside, I was completely unrecognizable with a white trench coat, a Seahawks cap, and mirrored sunglasses. I locked the Hummer and hurried inside. A few kids raised eyebrows at me from the kitchen, but no one stopped me. I sniffed the air and found Victoria and Soleil's scents. I followed them up the stairs and into a bedroom.

Victoria sat, doubled over on a bed which had been stripped of its sheets and blankets. I ran over to her. "Are you okay now?"

She shook her head. "This is worse than any of the other times."

"And she took a bunch of pain pills," Soleil added. "Help me zip this suitcase."

I kissed Victoria's cheek. Then I went over to Soleil and pressed down on the luggage. She zipped it all the way. "Thanks."

Victoria cried out in pain. My heart constricted, and I ran back over to the bed, cradling her. "We'll find the cure. I swear we will."

She moaned.

"Let's get this stuff loaded into the cars," Soleil said. "I get the feeling she's only going to get worse."

The familiar ache set into my bones, warning me of my impending shift. "You're right about that." I turned to Victoria. "Will you be okay here for a few minutes?"

She mumbled something and threw herself onto the mattress.

"We'll hurry."

All the bags and luggage were piled around near the door. I grabbed two, stuffed them under my arms, and then grabbed two more. Soleil followed me down the stairs and we loaded them into the Hummer, going back upstairs for a few more trips until we had everything tucked securely inside.

"Can you drive her car?" I asked. "I don't think she's up for it."

"Yeah, no problem."

We headed back to the room. Victoria sat up, breathing heavily. "Is that everything?"

Soleil nodded. "If it's not, Sasha will let you come back and take whatever you forgot."

"Do you want me to carry you?" I asked.

Victoria shook her head. "People will ask questions. I don't—ow!—want to bring any attention to you." She took a deep breath and stood.

I opened my mouth to protest.

"I'm okay, really." She held her hand against the wall and walked toward the door.

It killed me to see her in so much pain. Yes, some pain was normal during the course of a shift, but this was wrong. Not even a young, newly-shifting wolf would be in this much agony.

"Lean on me," I urged.

"I can do this." She kept her hand on the walls as she made her way to the stairs. When she took the first step, she stumbled. Her foot went underneath and her body thrust down toward the steps.

Soleil and I both lunged for her, catching her before she made contact. I wrapped my arm around her, holding her close. Soleil darted down ahead of us and glanced around. "Coast is clear. Hurry."

I scooped up Victoria and rushed toward the Hummer.

Soleil held up Victoria's purse. "I'm going to drive your car, okay?"

Moaning, Victoria nodded. I got her situated in the passenger seat of the Hummer and buckled her in. "Do you need anything before we head to Moonhaven?"

"Something to eat."

"That won't be a problem. Brick's been cooking all week, getting ready for the feast. We're all starving." I'd been eating nonstop all day, trying to stave off the bulk of my ravenous appetite. My stomach roared, just from me thinking about it.

I started the vehicle and peeled out. Victoria moaned and held her head.

"What can I do?" I asked.

"It's not you. It feels like my bones are going to break."

"Have they done that before?" I asked.

"Yes, but everything hurts more than—" She cried out.

My throat closed up. "Gessilyn's still at Moonhaven. Maybe she can come up with something to stop the pain, at least."

Victoria let loose a blood-curdling scream that made my ears hurt. It was so intense I had to pull over and cover my ears. After she stopped, I turned to her. She was drenched in sweat and gasping for air.

"We're almost there."

She nodded and leaned against the window. I pulled back into traffic and floored it, keeping my eyes open for cops. I weaved my way in and out of the lanes until I finally made it to our private road. Just a little longer. I remotely unlocked the gate before it came into view. I tore inside and squealed to a stop, spraying dirt and gravel. I left the gate open for Soleil. I'd left her in the dust somewhere just after pulling over.

"We're here."

Victoria moaned.

I ran around to her side and pulled her out. As I unbuckled the belt, she screamed. Something crunched.

"What was that?" I exclaimed.

"My leg!"

I scooped her up, and sure enough, her right leg twisted out at a funny angle. It was broken. Something else cracked.

She screamed, with tears running down her face.

"I'm getting you inside to Gessilyn."

Another crunch. She leaned her head against my chest and sobbed.

My heart constricted and my breath caught. I had to focus. She needed me now more than ever. I ran inside and set her on the couch in the living room.

She screamed again.

I took her hand. "Squeeze as hard as you can."

Victoria didn't even grasp it. "It's broken, too."

"Someone get in here!" I shouted as loud as I could.

Footsteps ran toward us from several directions. Brick, Sal, Jet, Ziamara, Dillon, Johan, Gessilyn, and Soleil all entered.

"We did burn the body," Johan called. He stared at us when he came into the room. "What's wrong?"

Victoria hollered again. I wiped sweat from her face with my jacket. That's when I remembered my outfit. I took off the cap and glasses and turned to everyone. "Her body's trying to shift, but can't."

She arched her back and cried out. Several pops sounded.

I shuddered. The wolf inside me fought to get out. "And I don't think I'm going to be able to hold off shifting. My wolf is going crazy."

Sharp pains ran throughout my body. It was going to be quick, and it was going to hurt—though probably nowhere as much as Victoria.

"I won't leave her side," Soleil said.

"And I'll see if I can find a spell to minimize the breaking and the pain," Gessilyn said.

Victoria lifted her head. "Are my bones... going to... go back?"

I had no idea, but couldn't let her know that. Ignoring my raging pain, I knelt down next to her and kissed her cheek. "Yes, as soon as we all shift back, so will you."

My wolf grew stronger. I clenched my teeth, trying not to focus on the pain. It was all happening so fast.

Victoria screamed, arching her back again.

In one quick, painful flash the shift started. I had no choice except to run from the room, unless I wanted to strip in front of everyone.

Without a word, I bolted outside and ran around to the back of the house, throwing off clothes as I went.

CHAPTER 19

Victoria

MY BODY FELT LIKE SOUP. I couldn't move anything, because every bone was broken—at least as far as I could tell. But at least the pain had subsided.

Howls sounded outside.

I gasped for air and looked around the room. Gessilyn sat at the end of the couch, flipping through an old book. Soleil stared at me, her eyes wide and face pale. For someone whose *job* was bringing death, she was pretty shaken.

"Did Toby shift?" I whispered.

Soleil nodded. "Do you need anything? Pain medication?"

Did I need anything? I couldn't even feel a thing, and that was a welcome relief. "I don't know."

"You look…" Her face contorted as though struggling with how to word the rest of her sentence.

"Like death?" I asked.

She frowned. "Worse. Maybe you should sleep."

Scratching sounded at the front door.

Soleil arched a brow. "I'm going to see what's going on. I'll be right back."

I tried to readjust myself, but could only move my head.

The tapping and scratching of claws sounded on the hardwood floor. A beautiful black and white wolf walked into the room. The top of his head and along his back was black. His face was mostly white and the rest of the fur blended, mixing the two colors.

Toby.

He walked over to the couch and leaned his head against me.

"I wish I could've shifted with you."

His wet nose tickled my skin, and then he licked my arm where it stuck out at a bad angle.

Soleil came in, followed by a tall, handsome man with light blue eyes who I didn't immediately recognize. He walked over to me, rubbed the fur between Toby's ears, and gave me a sad smile. "Hi, Victoria."

"Alex," I whispered.

"What happened?"

Toby stepped back and howled, the noise echoing around the room.

Howling sounded from outside as the rest of the pack beckoned him to join them.

"Victoria?" Alex said.

"I still can't shift. My bones—they…" Tears filled my eyes.

Soleil frowned, pain covering her own face. "Her bones are all broken."

Alex's eyes widened, his eyes seeming to turn a paler shade of blue. He turned to Soleil and then Gessilyn. "Can't you two do *something*?"

"I'm trying," Gessilyn said. "I've been trying. We have to try something new. It's a magic I'm not familiar with."

"Why not?"

"It has to do with the jaguars, and it's from Central America. I know nothing about their magic. Like dragon magic, it's a different beast from what I'm used to."

He turned to Soleil. "You can't help?"

She shook her head. "My powers go in the opposite direction. I take life, not heal it."

Alex looked deep in thought, then his face lit up.

Soleil arched a brow. "What?"

"Can you transfer life?"

"What do you mean?"

"I've seen how you suck the souls of—"

"I drink people's essence."

"But can you take it from one person and give it to another?"

Soleil tilted her head. "Where are you going with this?"

"Take some of mine and give it to her."

"I've never tried that." Soleil's brows came together. "I don't know what that would do." She tapped her temple and glanced up, looking deep in thought. "I don't recall hearing anything about that in school, either."

"Try it. Take mine and give it to her."

She took a deep breath. "I don't know. What if something goes wrong?"

"Couldn't you just suck it back out?"

"Drink."

"Try it," Alex urged. "We're both wolves, and I'm in human form, like she is."

"Wait," I said. "What if you get hurt in the process?"

"It's worth the risk. From what I've seen, each full moon is worse for you. We need to try it." He knelt down on one knee and looked to the ground. "You're the alpha wolfess of the pack. It's my honor to risk a sacrifice for you."

My heart raced. "But you've already done so much for me. All those times I met you in the woods before I remembered anything about werewolves—"

"Let me do this for you." He glanced up and held my gaze.

"You probably should," Gessilyn said. "There's nothing in any of my books."

I glanced at Soleil. "What do you think?"

She shrugged. "Your guess is as good as mine."

Toby howled again.

It appeared that I had no other choice. I sighed. "Okay, but don't hurt Alex."

"I won't," Soleil said. "I'll start with just a little essence and see if it's even possible to transfer it to you."

"Thank you." I closed my eyes, too exhausted to keep them open. I heard the now-familiar sound of Soleil's wings popping out and felt the breeze of them moving around.

After a moment, she spoke, just inches from me. "Are you ready?"

I nodded. Then my mouth opened, and instead of feeling the pull, the silky feeling ran down my throat. My body convulsed, but I felt my bones grow stronger. They moved within me, regaining their proper shape. Everything tingled as the bones reconnected.

The silky feeling disappeared and my mouth shut, but the tingling continued. My bones were repairing themselves. I continued shaking and jolting, the tingling sensations turning into aches.

"Is she okay?" Alex asked.

Toby's wet nose nudged my arm.

Finally, my body went still—but not like before. I felt like I could stand. I opened my eyes to find everyone staring at me.

"Well?" Soleil asked.

"I think it worked." I pushed myself up to sitting. Everything seemed to be in its proper place.

"Can you stand?"

My heart thundered. "I'll try."

Toby moved closer to me and rested his head on my lap. I patted his fur and took a deep breath. He nudged me, as if trying to say he would catch me if I fell.

I lowered my legs to the floor and pressed the soles of my feet firmly against it. My pulse drummed in my ears. Toby nuzzled his nose under my hand, urging me to try.

Alex held out a hand. I took it and balanced myself by placing my other hand on the top of Toby's furry head. It was now or never. I forced myself to stand. My legs held my weight as though they hadn't just been broken moments earlier.

"It worked!" Soleil squealed. "It actually worked."

"What now?" I asked.

"Are you up to visiting the Faeble?" Gessilyn asked.

I turned to her, surprised. "The Faeble?"

She nodded. "There's nothing I can do for you. I may be the high witch, but I'm not all-powerful. Tap knows so many people I don't. Since we can't get to the jaguars, you're going to need to tap into his resources."

My legs wobbled. Toby moved closer to me and Alex wrapped his arm around my shoulders, steadying me.

"C-can't we just call him?" I asked.

"Or I can go," Alex said. "You stay here and rest."

"Just let me call him," Soleil said. "Get her into the kitchen. The girl needs to eat." She pulled out her phone and headed up the stairs. "Tap, old buddy. Are you up for a challenge? Because…" Her voice trailed off as she disappeared from sight.

Toby whined.

"Are you hungry?" Alex asked.

Though I'd eaten as much as I could all week to prepare for ravaging hunger, I was still famished. I nodded.

Alex tightened his grip around my shoulders. "Let's get you into the kitchen." He turned to Toby. "You can go outside. I'll make sure Victoria's okay."

Toby plunked his rear end on the floor.

I rubbed his fur. "I hear the pack howling for you."

He stared at me, his eyes piercing me to the soul.

"I love you, too. But they need you, and I'm in good hands with Gessilyn, Soleil, and Alex."

"Isn't Ziamara around, too?" Gessilyn asked.

I shook my head. "She usually stays awake all month and then sleeps while Jet's in wolf form."

"Can't say that I blame her. If I were a vampire married to a werewolf, I'd do the same. Since I've completely exhausted my resources, do you mind if I call on the vampire queen? She has far-reaching resources that I can't touch. Her son-in-law is a former dragon king."

Alex shook his head. "I can't believe all the inter-species marriages."

"It's a strange mix of the old world and new right now," Gessilyn agreed. She turned to me. "Do you mind if I involve the vampires?"

Toby whined.

I looked over at him. "Is that a whine of agreement or a protest?"

He whined again, and I still couldn't tell his intentions.

"If Tap can't help us," Gessilyn said, "then we'll be out of options, Toby."

Soleil ran down the stairs. "Tap says to bring her over." She glanced my way. "Are you up for a run through the woods, or should I transport you?"

"Can I eat first?"

"Yes, come on."

We all went into the kitchen. Alex kept me steady as I stumbled along.

I didn't want to make Soleil transport me—not knowing how much it took out of her—but on the other hand, if I could barely make it to the kitchen, how would I get to the Faeble?

Alex helped me sit at the table while Soleil piled some food on a plate and stuffed it in the microwave. Toby sat in front of me, under the table and rested his head on my lap.

Soleil turned to Gessilyn. "What do you think the vampires can do that Tap can't?"

"Not so much the vampires, but their resources run deep. The king is the firstborn of the species and is well over three thousand years old. His reach goes beyond anyone I know."

"Sounds like someone I need to acquaint myself with," Soleil said. The microwave beeped and she pulled out the steaming plate of food and placed it in front of me. "There's plenty if you want more."

I grabbed a fork and shoveled the food in, not caring what I ate. My stomach raged, begging for as much as possible.

After my third plate, I was finally satiated—not full, but at least not hungry. Alex sat across from me. "Are you up for a trip through the woods?"

"There's only one way to find out."

"If you can't make it, I'll carry you. Bring you back here, like I did last time."

"Let's do it."

A whine sounded underneath the table. I rubbed Toby's fur. "It'll be okay. You can go with us if you want."

My bones still held a minor ache, but it was nothing like it had been. I just hoped that my bones didn't break all over again when it was time to shift back—I was already human. My body wouldn't need to shift into anything, but did it know that?

CHAPTER 20

Toby

I RAN THROUGH THE WOODS, following Victoria and the others. It didn't sit right with me that they wanted to bring the vampires into any of this. It could only lead to problems... or was I only being selfish?

The queen and I'd had a relationship many decades earlier—long before she was queen and when Victoria had been dead for many years. Our past had never been awkward before, but now with Victoria back, I could hardly live with myself, thinking about my one brief indiscretion. I should have never allowed my heart to leave Victoria for even a moment, death or not.

We made it to the Faeble, and I paced outside. Short of an emergency, Tap wanted his patrons in human form when inside. If all of Victoria's bones had still been broken inside of her, I would have insisted. But now I had no excuse and was left only with my guilt.

She doesn't hold it against you, my wolf told me.

Doesn't matter. I know, and I have to live with it.

She had her thing with Carter, don't forget.

Thanks, I appreciate the reminder. I paced the length of the building.

You have nothing to feel guilty over. She was dead. *The vampire was close to death—well, the second death—and you helped her through that. Look at how much good has happened under her leadership. She needed you to get through that rough patch.*

No amount of logic could convince me that I shouldn't feel guilty. I'd promised Victoria that it would always be her, and for a short time, it wasn't.

I glanced over at the building. What was taking them so long? Could it mean that Tap had some ideas, and that we wouldn't need to contact the vampires?

The thought of introducing the two of them made my stomach lurch. There had to be another way—and I would find it.

You're the only one who holds this against you.

I ignored my wolf, who I knew wanted to check on the rest of the pack, but neither of us wanted to go too far from Victoria. As much as I wanted her to be able to shift, he wanted it all the more.

Even if we have to bring in the vampires, everything will be fine. Everyone has moved on and she's married with ten or eleven children.

Easy for you to say, I snapped. *You weren't unfaithful.*

He shook our head. *You're impossible sometimes. In protecting yourself, you're hurting her now. She doesn't care— nobody does, except you.*

I couldn't respond. He was right. I might have to accept the fact that the only way to save Victoria was by facing my own demons. But there was still time. I would find another way. I would.

At least that's something. Don't wait too long.

We continued pacing. Anger surged through me, as I thought about whoever had done this to her—more than likely the jaguars with either my father or hers behind the whole thing. I would deal with every last one of them once Victoria was restored to her natural state.

Several wolves howled in the distance. They had gone farther than the bar. From the sounds of it, they were on the other side of the immense woods.

When would the shift finally be over? I needed to be inside with Victoria, and being unable to help her was the worst kind of torture.

As I paced, now around the entire bar, the rest of the pack continued howling. They wanted me to join them, but at least I knew they understood why I couldn't.

Hopefully this'll be the last full moon the pack won't be together, my wolf told me.

If it wasn't, I didn't know what that would mean for her. With each one growing worse than the last, I couldn't see her surviving another full moon.

My wolf didn't disagree.

Maybe running with the pack will help clear our head.

I stopped pacing. *I'm not leaving Victoria.*

I didn't say to leave her. Just to go for a run. She's well taken care of in there.

Irritation burned at me. If he was a separate entity, I'd have been tempted to attack.

Easy there, he warned.

I sure was glad he remained quiet the rest of the month.

You just don't notice me.

Growling, I burst into a run. I stayed close enough that I'd hear Victoria the moment she stepped outside.

The exercise felt good on my muscles, and it was a good distraction. Time seemed to stand still, but as I glanced up at the moon, I could see it moving slowly across the sky.

Finally, the ache set in. I headed back for the Faeble and shifted into human form mid-stride. It took my feet only a moment to adjust and I headed for the back of the building for my spare clothes.

They were gone.

I stared at my little cubby-hole in disbelief. I'd checked my stock not long ago. Someone had borrowed from it and not replaced the clothes? I groaned and moved over to the other cubbies. Jet was the only one who had multiple sets of clothes, and unfortunately, he was not my build.

Muttering, I slid on the too-short pants and shirt. I rolled up the sleeves to my elbows, giving the illusion of an okay fit. The pants on the other hand... I sighed. Not only did I have no shoes, but the cuffs rested well above my ankles.

I went inside. Loud music and conversation greeted me. I went to the bar. Quinn was busy making a drink, but Tap and the others were nowhere to be seen.

A bitter scent wafted over. I glanced over at a table next to me, the group of sirens burst into a fit of laughter, pointing at some mesmers a few tables over.

"Where's the flood?" one asked me. They all laughed harder. It was a stupid joke, but sirens loved hating werewolves.

I ignored them and caught Quinn's attention from behind the bar. "Where's Tap?"

"They went downstairs."

"Thanks." I hurried down to the basement. It was Tap's living quarters—a rich mixture of the old world and the new.

Victoria and the others weren't in the front room, so I went down the hall, looking into the other rooms. They were in the same room we'd been in when Gessilyn ran the spell to restore Victoria's memories.

"What's going on?" I glanced around the room, not seeing Victoria. "Where is she?"

"Sleeping," Soleil said. "Nice outfit."

"Why's she asleep?" I demanded. Finally, I saw her, lying on a decorative rug, covered in blankets. Alex was curled up next to her. "What happened?"

Tap unbuttoned his top two buttons and loosened his shirt. "I was trying an ancient remedy my people have relied on for centuries, when she started screaming."

I grimaced. "Did her bones break again?"

Soleil nodded. "I transferred Alex's essence to her again. It kept the rest of her bones from breaking and healed the ones that already did again, but it made both of them fall asleep."

I turned to Tap. "What are we going to do? She can't go through this again."

"We'll figure something out. I'm going to pore over my ancient books. In the meantime, contact the spice shop. See what Old Willy and his son know."

"I already cashed in on the favor he owes you, remember?"

Tap nodded. "And now you know him. You have an in."

I groaned. "He wasn't too happy about helping us out last

time."

"They're always like that. Don't take it personally."

"Are we just going to let them sleep?" I asked.

"I would," Gessilyn said. "The shift took a lot out of her and the essence exchange wiped out Alex."

"We need to find a cure for her right now." I paced the length of the room.

"I can contact the vampires," Gessilyn said.

"Thanks," I said.

"And I'll go to the spice shop," Soleil said. "If he gets grouchy, I'll find a way to convince him to help."

"I'm sure you will. I'm staying with Victoria."

"Good," Tap said. "You can help me read through my books."

Gessilyn and Soleil left. Tap pulled half a dozen thick, old books from a shelf. He handed me half the stack. "Let's get to work."

"What are we looking for, exactly?" I asked.

"A way to reverse her curse."

I dropped the books onto the table. "And how will I know it when I see it?"

"Pay close attention."

"Great," I muttered.

"It's not that bad. My people have always taken great notes."

We made ourselves comfortable and I flipped through the brown pages with fading ink. The book appeared to have no order. One page held history, the next a recipe, the following one a spell. Someone needed to organize and update them, but I wasn't going to suggest it to the proud little troll.

After a while, he glanced at me. "Find anything?"

"More history than spells."

"Did you notice the history is full of information that could help with spells?"

"*Could* being the operative word."

Quinn came in, his eyes wild. "We need you, Tap. Some sirens and mesmers have gotten into a brawl."

Tap scowled. "They know better than to do that in here." He rose and headed for the door before turning back to me. "I'll be back. In the meantime, keep reading."

I nodded and flipped another page, keeping an eye on Victoria from the corner of my vision. She and Alex both slept heavily. I was grateful to him for keeping such a close eye on her when I could do so very little as a wolf. It had to be miserable only being able to shift into human form once a month. Once we got everything squared away with her, we'd have focus on breaking the curse for the rest of us, particularly for his sake.

My eyes grew heavy as I flipped through the old pages, finding nothing to help Victoria.

After a while, Brick and Dillon entered the room.

"There you are," Brick said.

"We kept calling your phone," Dillon said, "but then we realized it was outside."

I nodded toward the books. "Start reading. We only have a month to break Victoria's curse—and the time is going to race by all too fast."

They took a seat, and for a while, the only sounds in the room were of the pages flipping.

Footsteps sounded in the hall. I glanced toward the door,

hoping either Gessilyn or Soleil had found something that would lead us to a cure.

Quinn appeared, looking more frazzled than before. "Where's Tap?"

"I haven't seen him since you were last down here."

His face paled. "Tap's gone."

CHAPTER 21

Toby

I STARED AT QUINN. "WHAT do you mean, he's *gone*?"

"He helped me with that scuffle between the sirens and the mesmers. After things calmed down, he went outside to take the trash out. I was so distracted with making and serving the drinks that I didn't realize he hadn't come back in."

"How long ago was that?" I exclaimed. "Did he come back in?"

Quinn frowned. "I don't know. I was busy for hours. It wasn't until things calmed down up there that I noticed."

"Did you try calling him?" Brick asked.

"His phone is behind the bar."

I took a deep breath. "There has to be a logical explanation."

"Yeah," Dillon said. "Do you think the jaguars got to him, too? If our suspicions are right, they've imprisoned their leader's own son. Why not Tap?"

Brick pulled out his phone. "I'm calling Soleil."

"What's she going to do?" Dillon asked.

"Kill those bastards. She's taken out entire villages before. Those feline idiots will be nothing."

Dillon frowned. "But if they hold the key to Victoria's cure, killing them won't do any good."

"Then she can kill some key players and demand what we need." Brick scrolled around his screen and put the phone up to his ear. "She's not answering."

"Maybe she's busy talking with Darrell at the spice shop," I said. "That's where Tap sent her."

Brick shook his head. "It's not like her to miss my calls." He slid his finger around the screen again and brought it back to his ear.

Dillon and I exchanged a worried glance.

Brick swore. "Where *is* she?"

"I've never seen you like this," Dillon said.

"Soleil's never been missing before," Brick grumbled.

"He rarely gets violent," I said. "But mess with someone he cares about and it's a different story. The last guy who threatened me ended up in a wheelchair."

Dillon grimaced.

Brick slammed his fist on the table. "She's still not answering. Something's up. No one can reach Soleil, Tap, or Carter. There's no way it's all a coincidence."

"No, it's not." I clenched my fists.

"What are we going to do?" Quinn asked, his eyes wide.

I glanced over at Victoria. "I'm not leaving her side—not with everyone disappearing."

"Why are they all disappearing?" Quinn asked. "What's going on?"

"They all have one thing in common." My nostrils flared.

"What?" Quinn exclaimed.

I glanced over at Victoria. "They were all helping her. So

was I when I was abducted."

Quinn glanced back and forth between Victoria and me. "You're going to have to explain that later."

I nodded, and he went back up to the bar.

"So, you agree with Brick that it's got to be the jags?" Dillon asked.

"It's worth looking into. We can't rule anything out yet."

Brick jumped from his chair, nearly knocking over the table. "And we know exactly where they are. I say we storm the place."

"No," I said, staring into his eyes.

He squirmed while staring at me. "I mean no offense, sir, but this is an emergency."

"I realize that—and that's the exact reason we need a *plan*."

Brick turned away. "Easy for you to say. Your girlfriend is right here."

"Excuse me?" I was in shock. My friend had never spoken that way to me before.

He turned back to me. "Soleil is missing. I can't just sit around and do nothing."

I stepped toward him, narrowing my eyes. "Victoria will die if we don't handle this correctly. One more full moon without the ability to shift will surely kill her. We're not jumping into anything blind."

"What are we going to do, then?" Brick stepped closer to me. "Like I said, I'm not going to do nothing."

"And we won't. All of these abductions are related. If we all think with clear heads, we'll be able to figure this out. Another thing—no one goes anywhere alone. None of us. I'm going to wake Victoria. One of you call Moonhaven and tell the others what's going on."

Dillon glanced at Victoria. "Uh, do you think it's such a good idea to bring her back with us?"

Anger twisted through my gut. "What do you mean?"

"If all the abductions—"

"Moonhaven is her home. End of discussion. Call the others before anyone else disappears." I marched over to Victoria and brushed some hair away from her eyes. "Wake up, sweetness."

She stirred, but didn't wake. In the background, Dillon argued with Brick about calling Moonhaven.

I turned toward them and made an executive decision. "Brick, you make the call." I hated being like that—it reminded me too much of my father—but sometimes I had to play hardball. I turned back toward Victoria and ran the back of my fingers along her face. "We need to get going. Wake up."

Her eyes fluttered and then opened. She looked around and sat up. "What's going on? Where am I?"

"At the Faeble. We need to get to Moonhaven."

Victoria rubbed her eyes. "Did Tap find anything? I couldn't stay awake." She frowned.

"Tap and Soleil..." I paused, not wanting to upset her. "They aren't here right now. Come on." I held my hand out to help her up.

"Where'd they go?"

"That's the million-dollar question," Dillon muttered.

Victoria gave me a confused glance.

"They've gone missing."

Her eyes widened and she scrambled to her feet. "What happened?"

"I don't think it's a coincidence that we can't find them or Carter."

"You think they're at the Jag?"

"It's a good possibility."

She turned to Alex. "Time to get up!"

The wolf raised his head and looked around.

Brick came over to us. "I just got off the phone with Jet. He's going to tell everyone else to stick together."

Victoria grabbed onto my arm. "Is all of this because of me? Everyone who's tried to find my cure has been abducted—right after my college funds were cut."

"Or they want me," I said. "The jaguars used you as bait to get to me, right?"

Her eyes shone with tears. "What do they want with us?"

"I don't know, but I intend to find out. We need to get back home."

The five of us, including Alex, hurried out of the Jag. Quinn raced out after us. "What are we going to do?"

"Just take care of the Faeble," I told him. "That's what Tap would want—to come back to it exactly as he left it."

"I can't run it on my own, and besides, I want to help find Tap, too."

"We have to get to Moonhaven," I said. "Find someone to help you while Tap is gone. We'll find him. I swear to it."

Quinn frowned. "Okay, but I don't like it. I'd rather be actively searching."

"Tap wants his beloved business to be run by someone capable who cares. That would be you. You have my number?"

"Yeah." He sighed.

"And I have yours." Something crashed inside. "You'd

better get in there before the customers get rowdy."

Quinn hurried inside. The rest of us broke into a run, heading home.

Once inside, Brick turned to me. "I want to go to the spice shop and look around for Soleil. Even if she isn't there, we might find clues, but time is of the essence."

"You're right. Who do you want to take?"

"Sal, but that would leave you without either of your bodyguards, sir."

"Take him," I said. "The rest of the pack and a family of witches are here. We'll be fine." I hoped. "Just don't split up—not even for a moment."

He nodded. "We won't."

"And if you see anything remotely suspicious, give me a call."

"Yes, sir." He ran up the stairs.

I turned to Victoria. "Do you need to rest some more?"

She shook her head, but her expression told me otherwise. Dark bands sat under her puffy, bloodshot eyes.

"I beg to differ." I leaned in and kissed her softly on the lips. "Do you like the purple room? I had you in mind when we decorated that one."

Her mouth formed a weak smile. "I love it, but—"

"But nothing. You need your rest after the shift tonight. I'll bring your things in, but first, we need to find Ziamara. I want her in the room with you. Like I said, none of us is to be alone."

She arched a brow. "Not even you, right?"

"That's correct." I turned away from her and listened. It sounded like Jet and Ziamara were in the living room. "Jet!

Ziamara! Come here!"

They ran over, and I explained everything. Ziamara helped Victoria up the stairs. Jet and I went outside to load Victoria's things into her new room.

"I'll put your things away," Ziamara told Victoria. "You get some sleep. I won't need any for about a month, so I won't take my eyes off her."

I kissed Victoria's forehead. "Listen to her and rest."

She nodded and leaned against me. "I'm sorry I brought all this into the pack."

My heart shattered. "You did no such thing. It was those jaguars—and our fathers are probably behind them. Once again, we're stuck in their crossfire. It's no fault of yours, do you understand?"

Victoria sighed. "I guess so."

"You'll feel better after some more sleep." I pulled the covers up, and she climbed in. "I'm going to be downstairs if you need me, and Ziamara isn't going anywhere."

She shook her head. "I'm just going to be unpacking as quietly as possible."

"Thanks." Victoria leaned onto the pillow and closed her eyes.

I gave her a quick kiss and tucked the blankets around her. "Sweet dreams."

Jet wrapped his arms around Ziamara and stared into her eyes, probably thinking sweet nothings that only she could hear. I gave them a moment and then waved Jet over into the hall.

He followed me downstairs. "What are we going to do?"

"We're going to have to find a way into the Jag. I'm certain that's where they're holding Tap and the others."

"I don't suppose you know anyone who can get in there?"

"Unfortunately, no."

We went into the living room, where everyone else had gathered.

"Is Victoria okay?" Nora asked.

I nodded. "She's resting now with Ziamara." I glanced around the group. "In case you didn't hear—we're using the buddy system. Nobody so much as pees alone, got it?"

Everyone nodded, but some grumbled.

"I'm serious. Not only have Victoria and I been taken by the jaguars, but now they've also managed to get Carter, Soleil, and Tap. One of their own, an angel of death, and a troll king. We're not dealing with amateurs. They're probably behind that cursed dead body, and they very likely hold the key to Victoria's cure."

"Can't we find a doctor to remove the mole?" Dillon asked. "No mole, no curse, right?"

"I don't know if it's that simple," I said. "We don't know what kind of magic we're dealing with here. Our focus is on getting inside the Jag—using the buddy system. Nobody goes in alone."

"The vampire royalty offered their assistance," Gessilyn said. "You just have to tell them what you need."

Relief washed through me. As much as I worried about seeing the queen, we needed their assistance. "The entire group is going to help?"

"If needed, yes."

"Gessilyn, you come with me. We need to discuss the vampires. The rest of you, brainstorm ideas. We need as many as possible."

CHAPTER 22

Victoria

I WOKE UP FEELING RESTED, which was nothing short of a miracle after the horrible almost-shift I'd endured. I stretched and opened my eyes. Ziamara stood by the window, looking out. Bright sunlight shone into the room, indicating it was late morning.

My things had taken over the room. She'd put up pictures of Toby and me everywhere. My laptop and backpack sat at the desk. My clothes hung in the closet.

All of that meant I could see Toby every day, and that was something I'd wanted for as long as I could remember.

It was too bad I likely only had until the next full moon. I couldn't see surviving it unless I could actually shift. My bones still ached a little where they had broken and later healed.

Ziamara turned to me and smiled. "You're awake. I hope you're hungry."

"Hungry?"

"Toby's insisting we don't let the jaguars make us miss Thanksgiving. Those boys love any opportunity to feast." She smiled.

I sniffed the air. I could smell turkey roasting and a mixture of side dishes cooking, too.

"I'm going to get a shower before heading downstairs. Thanks for organizing the room."

"No problem. It wasn't like I had anything else to do, anyway. Oh, and if you don't like where anything is, just move it. You're not going to hurt my feelings."

"I'm sure it's fine." And I might only need the room for a month. My throat closed up at the thought, but I needed to come to terms with it. If we couldn't find the cure, this would be my last month with Toby.

Ziamara's expression turned to concern. "What's wrong?"

"Nothing," I said quickly.

"Don't make me read your thoughts."

I stared at her.

"Don't worry, I don't intrude on anyone's private thoughts—unless I need to. What's the matter?"

"Promise not to say anything to Toby?"

"Only if you promise *to* tell him."

I sighed. "I'm sure I'll have to, but I need to deal with the fact that…" My lips trembled and tears stung my eyes. "I might not live through the next shift."

Her eyes became as wide as saucers. "You can't give up."

"I'm going to fight with everything I have, but at the same time—"

"Let's get you in that shower. Toby says nobody can be alone at all, but I'll keep my back turned. Grab some clothes."

I sighed. "Have they made any progress?"

"Some of the royal vampires are coming. My adoptive parents might come, too." She hugged herself.

"Remind me who they are again." I pulled some clothes

from the closet.

"The king and queen. I haven't seen them in so long!"

I tried to smile. "That'll be really great. I bet you miss them."

"I do. I've hardly seen them since I left the castle."

"Do you think they'll be able to help us?" I headed for the bathroom.

Ziamara followed me. "They're really powerful, and they've fought all kinds of creatures. I'll bet the jaguars are nothing for them."

"So, they can defeat them. Do you think they can get them to give up the cure?"

"They can be really convincing—and scary."

"I guess we'll see." I set my clothes on the counter and started the shower.

She turned her back to me and sat on the toilet lid. "I'll just be on my phone. Forget I'm here."

"It doesn't bother me." I slid my clothes off and stepped into the stream of hot water.

My mind wandered to my missing friends. I hoped Toby and the guys had come up with something while I slept. The jaguars needed to be taken down. I may not have had any control over whether I could shift, but at least I could put my effort into finding and helping my friends.

Tears filled my eyes, blurring my vision. Toby and I had just reunited. It wasn't fair. Why couldn't we just get married and have our life together?

I turned the shower off. Ziamara handed me a towel around the shower curtain. I dried off and then got dressed while she played a game on her phone with her back turned toward me.

"Okay, I'm safe now." I toweled off my hair.

Ziamara turned around. "You ready to go downstairs and find out what the boys have been doing all this time?"

"They haven't checked in?" I ran a brush through my hair and looked in the mirror. My skin was pretty pale—not surprising given the ordeal I was recovering from.

"Nope. I could hear them discussing everything, but that's it."

I grabbed my clothes from the floor and went back to the bedroom. My bedroom—for as long as that lasted. A lump formed in my throat at the thought of not surviving the next full moon. I blinked back tears as I put on makeup.

Once I was done, we headed downstairs. Everyone was gathered around the kitchen table, eating and discussing eviscerating jaguars.

"Any news?" I asked.

Toby turned around. His face lit up when he saw me. He jumped up from his seat and wrapped his arms around me. "How do you feel?" He pressed his lips on mine, tasting of bacon and donuts.

"Rested. Did you guys learn anything?"

"Not a whole lot, but some of the vampires are on their way." He helped me sit in an empty chair next to his.

Jet held out a chair for Ziamara. "There's no way that anything could go wrong with that."

"They respect Toby," Brick said. "And we'll respect them."

Toby piled some breakfast food on my plate.

"But no news about Tap or Soleil or Carter?" I asked.

He shook his head sadly. "Nothing."

Anger surged through me.

"The vampires are supposed to sneak in and find out," Dillon said.

"When are they supposed to get here?" I bit into a piece of bacon.

"They have some things to wrap up first," Toby said. "They should be here in a day or two."

I thought of our friends languishing in the jaguar torture cells. "That's too long. What about the witches?" I glanced around, realizing none of them were there.

"They're sleeping," Dillon said.

"What about the vampires? Don't they have their own witches?" I ate some eggs, finding that my appetite was waning quickly.

Toby put his arm around me. "They're working on it. We'll have a huge advantage over the jaguars. Don't worry, okay?"

"Easier said than done." The question was whether I would still be on this side of death's door once everything was done.

Toby leaned closer. "Are you sure you're okay?" he whispered, tickling my ear.

I started to nod, but stopped. "No. How could I be?" I put the fork down on the plate.

He put his arm around me. "I'm going outside with Victoria if anyone needs me."

We went outside and sat on the swinging bench.

"What's going on?" he asked.

"Besides our three missing friends and the fact that we only have a month together?"

His eyes widened. "What? No. We're going to get to the bottom of this. We're going to shift together come the next full moon."

I arched a brow. "You're really that sure?"

"There aren't any other options. With the vampires' help, we're going to work with all kinds of witches we wouldn't otherwise have access to. The jaguars are going to regret ever going near us."

"But if Gessilyn is the high witch, can the other ones really offer us anything she can't?"

He kissed my forehead. "Of course. She's strong, but her knowledge is low—she's completely new to the role. Nobody knew she was the high witch until last summer. Some of the witches the vampires are rounding up are ancient. They've been practicing for thousands of years. Between their experience and Gessilyn's power, we're going to see magic unlike any other."

"I hope you're right."

His eyes filled with concern and ran his fingers through my hair. "I won't let you die again."

"Marry me tonight." I pulled out my necklace and took the ring off, sliding it onto my finger, where it belonged. "We may as well make the most of this month."

His jaw dropped and he shook his head. "You can't think like this. Next month, you're going to shift and finally let your wolf free. We'll run together. Then we'll plan the biggest, most beautiful wedding anyone has ever seen and follow that with a glorious months-long honeymoon."

"What if it doesn't work out that way, Toby?" I gazed into his deep blue eyes.

"It *will*."

"But say it doesn't. Wouldn't you rather we at least spent

our last month together married? Or would you rather spend it with me sleeping in the lavender room and you in yours?"

"You think I'm sleeping before your curse is removed?"

My heart ached at what this was doing to him. Perhaps it was time to face the reality I didn't want to accept. "Maybe a happy ending isn't our fate. Let's at least have this month."

He swallowed. "I won't have you talking this way. We have to fight—harder than ever. Then we'll prove fate wrong and have centuries to spend together. Think of how much more we'll appreciate our time together after beating these odds."

I frowned, trying to keep my heart from shattering into a million pieces. "So, you won't give me this for my last month?"

"It isn't your last month!"

"You and I both know it may very well be. Please, Toby. Marry me now."

He trembled. "I refuse to think like that, and I don't want you to, either. We're going to get through this."

I fell against him, my heart breaking.

CHAPTER 23

Toby

I SAT ON THE EDGE of the bed and ran my hands over Victoria's hair as she slept.

"Is she okay?" Ziamara asked, her eyes wide with concern. "Should she be sleeping this much?"

"I think being unable to shift is really taking its toll." It had been three days since the full moon, and she'd slept about half the time.

"When are the other vampires getting here? They'll be able to help. I know it."

I glanced at the time. "I would think soon, though it'll depend on their method of travel. They're leaving Iceland."

"Hopefully, they'll take the dragon tunnels. Those are usually faster than the jets."

"Assuming all the dragons are friendly. Some of the cities don't like non-dragons traveling through." I kissed Victoria's cheek and glanced out the window. It was growing dark. "Maybe I should call them."

"I can do that," Ziamara offered.

"Thank you. I'm going to head downstairs."

When I got downstairs, half the pack was gathered in the

living room with Gessilyn and her family. Conversation drifted in from the kitchen, where the rest of the pack was gathered.

I stood next to the roaring fire.

"How is she?" Gessilyn asked.

"Sleeping."

Outside, Alex howled. A familiar, slightly bitter odor settled in the air. I hurried over to a front window. The vampires had arrived, and they stood outside the gate. "They're here!"

Some growls sounded.

I spun around. "They're here to help. Anyone who acts unbecomingly will deal with me—and you won't enjoy it. Got it?" I made eye contact with each werewolf in the room. They each nodded in agreement. "Good."

Alex howled again.

I hurried outside, running past the wolf to the gate. About a dozen vampires stood on the other side of my property, all dressed as elegantly as the royalty always did. I broke into a run, and so did Alex, staying by my side.

"Hold on," I called. When I reached the gate, I pressed the code to open it.

The vampires hurried in and I closed it behind them.

The queen wrapped me in a warm embrace. Her thick, regal robe stuck to my arm. "It's so good to see you again, Toby. I love your new place."

I returned the hug. Guilt wracked me. With Victoria alive again, would I ever be able to forgive myself for my short romantic relationship? "It's great to see you as well, Alexis."

She stepped back and smiled at her husband, Alrekur. "Actually, I go by my first name now. Marguerite."

"It's lovely," I said. "Follow me inside."

Once we were the in the house, Sal and Brick helped the guests by taking their coats.

"Come out," I called to everyone.

The pack and Gessilyn's family came into the entryway from the kitchen and living room.

Gessilyn greeted all the vampires with an embrace.

I cleared my throat. "Let me make the introductions." I placed my hand on the queen's shoulder. "This is Queen Marguerite and her husband, King Alrekur." I turned to the couple next to them. "This is his brother, Soren and his wife, Svana. I'm not sure who the others are."

"Tell us what you know," Alrekur said, not giving us time to finish introductions.

"Let's make ourselves comfortable in the living room," I said. "Are any of you thirsty? Hungry?"

The king shook his head. "We feasted on the way over."

I cringed, thinking of how many humans it would take to feed all those vampires.

"We didn't kill anyone." He laughed. "We found a hotel full of sleeping patrons and snacked."

Dillon shook his head. "Turning humans into vampires?"

"We just snack. They won't even notice the loss of blood, much less turn into a vampire."

"Follow me." I led them to the living room, and gestured for the guests to sit. Brick and Sal brought in extra chairs. Once everyone was settled, I filled them in on everything from the missing people to Victoria's curse.

Marguerite turned to me. "Where is she?"

"Sleeping. Not being able to turn is taking a real toll on

her."

"Poor thing." Marguerite frowned. "I can't wait to meet her."

"Let's head upstairs. Ziamara's with her."

Her eyes lit up. "How is my daughter?"

"Great. Very happy with Jet."

She turned to Alrekur. "You want to come up with me?"

He shook his head and kissed her hand. "You all catch up. I'm going to make some calls."

Marguerite and I headed upstairs.

"Are you okay?" she asked, looking me in the eyes once we reached the second level.

"My fiancée is under a curse and two friends are missing."

Her brows came together. "I thought three were missing."

"Yes, but to call the third my friend would be a stretch."

"Understood, but I get the feeling something else is bothering you."

As if the guilt eating me wasn't enough, she could read me like a book.

"Toby, talk to me. You've helped me through plenty of rough times, let me help you."

Her words were like a dagger in my heart. I nodded toward some plush chairs underneath a portrait of the Peninsula. She sat in one and I took the other.

She tilted her head. "What's wrong?"

"This is kind of awkward." I sighed and stared a mark on the wall across from us.

"I promise not to judge."

"No, I mean having you here."

Her mouth gaped. "I'm awkward?"

"That's not what I mean. You're..." My voice trailed off as images from our time together played in my mind. She'd been a young, depressed high school student, abandoned by every vampire she knew. I was her teacher and had only been trying to help pull her out of her funk. Somehow, we had temporarily filled the holes in each other's hearts.

"I don't understand," she said, bringing me back to the present. "Everything has always been good between us. Did I do something?"

I met her gaze. "Remember when your parents banished you from the castle and you couldn't contact any of the vampires?"

"Right. I... Oh!" Her eyes widened with marked understanding. "Oh, I see what you mean. Well, I'm not going to say anything about that to her. And also, don't forget you and Alre have always gotten along. Same thing."

"It's not." I shook my head, guilt squeezing my chest. How had I allowed myself to forget about Victoria?

Marguerite put her hand on mine. "It was so long ago, and now you have your second chance with the love of your life. You've finally found happiness again—and I couldn't be more thrilled for you. No one deserves it more." The look in her eyes told me she meant it wholly. "Can I meet her?"

Tears stung my eyes as I recalled Victoria begging me to marry her right away. How could she give in to the thought of only have this month to live?

"Toby? Are you okay?"

I couldn't look at the queen. "Do you think you can find a witch to help her?" My voice cracked. I'd managed to hold myself together so well in front of everyone else, but now with her there with me, my walls crumbled. I couldn't hold myself together anymore.

She frowned and wrapped her arms around me. "We can beat this. After all the things I've seen over the years, I have no doubt. My daughter, Eylin, is searching for a hard-to-reach, extremely powerful dragon witch. She's done things no one else could. And for what it's worth, I'm glad to finally help you after all the times you've helped me."

"It was nothing. But thank you, and I hope you're right." I rose. Somehow, I needed to push my guilt aside. It had been years ago and didn't mean anything now. I cleared my throat. "Let's get in there. Victoria's probably sleeping, but Zia's in there with her."

Her eyes lit up. "I can't wait to see her. Thank you so much for taking care of her."

"She's a delight. Truly."

I led her into the room Victoria was staying in. Sure enough, she slept, but Ziamara sat near the bed, reading. Her eyes widened when she saw our guest. Then she threw the book down and jumped into the queen's embrace. "I've missed you."

"As have I, child. You look well."

"I am. I love the pack. How's Larus?"

"Well—and downstairs, actually. He was eager to see how you're doing."

Ziamara looked at me, her eyes wide. She and Larus had an interest in each other at one point, years earlier.

I shrugged, knowing the awkwardness of former relationships all too well. The only two women I'd ever harbored any romantic feelings for were both in this bedroom.

Zia and her adoptive mother caught up, while I sat at the edge of the bed and ran my fingers through Victoria's hair.

Her eyes fluttered open. She seemed confused and then her gaze settled on me. "Toby, what's going on?"

I kissed her cheek. "The vampires are here. Everyone is eager to remove the curse from you."

She sat up and looked around. "Is that...?"

"The queen."

Victoria looked back and forth between her and me and bit her lip. "She's the one?"

I nodded, wanting to tell her that Marguerite meant nothing to me, but that wasn't entirely the truth. I just didn't care about her in the same way that I did Victoria. There was no way of putting it into words, especially with the both of them right there, so I wrapped my arms around her and took possession of her mouth and deepened the kiss. She returned the kiss greedily, clinging to me.

"You're awake!" Ziamara exclaimed. "You have to meet my mother. She saved my life by turning me into a vampire."

Victoria climbed out of bed and walked over to them. She shook the queen's hand. "I'm Victoria. It's a pleasure to meet you."

Marguerite threw her arms around Victoria, wrapping her in a tight hug. "The pleasure is all mine, sweetie. Toby's told me so much about you. I'm so glad you're alive, and you can rest assured I'll do everything in my power to keep it that way." She stepped back and looked Victoria over, beaming. "You're just as beautiful as he described. I just couldn't be happier that you two are reunited."

"I... thank you. It means a lot."

"Do you want to come downstairs and meet everyone?"

"Yes, let's go."

I sighed in relief. Maybe my guilt *had* been unfounded—especially if the vampires could help find a cure for Victoria's curse.

CHAPTER 24

Victoria

MY STRENGTH WAS WEAKENING BY the moment. I had to sleep constantly. Every time I went up to the room to sleep, someone had to come up with me because Toby still didn't want anyone going off alone—not even the vampires. Anyone working with us was in danger. So, I had started sleeping on the couches as everyone else discussed the plans so that nobody would be stuck watching me rest.

I woke in Toby's office and the entire place was quiet. I glanced around, at first not seeing anyone. A moment of panic struck me, but then I noticed Toby at his desk behind the computer screen.

"What's going on?" I asked.

He came over and pulled me into his lap, holding me tightly. "Everyone else left for the Jag. Some of the vampires are going to sneak inside while the werewolves wait, watching."

My stomach twisted in knots. "I hope they find Carter, Tap, and Soleil."

"You and me both." He kissed my cheek.

"Why didn't you go? As pack leader, I would have thought—"

"That the pack wolfess is my number one priority? You're right."

My heart fluttered. "But, still. You should be out there."

"It's for times like this that I have an assistant alpha. Jet loves leading, and he does a great job. I just want to be here with you." He ran the back of his fingers along my jawline and pressed his mouth against mine. He tasted minty, and I deepened the kiss. Then exhaustion ran through me like a freight train. I pulled back.

He cupped my head. "What's wrong?"

Aches ran through me. "I need to lay down."

Toby helped me. "This is only getting worse, isn't it?"

"Seems so." I closed my eyes, feeling him slip from me as I drifted away from consciousness.

He spoke in the background, but I couldn't make out a word he said.

A thick blanket of sleep overtook me.

CHAPTER 25

Toby

I TUCKED THE QUILT AROUND Victoria and adjusted the pillow. It was hard not to worry, especially since we were no closer to finding her cure.

Nervous energy ran through me. I got up and paced.

What was taking the vampires so long? They hadn't gotten caught, had they? The king—the most powerful vampire in existence—and his brother had gone in with a couple other royals. The queen, my pack, and the remaining vampires were supposed to be spread strategically throughout the woods, surrounding the Jag, ready to jump in and fight if need be.

But what if the jaguars found the vampires? Could they overtake them? I'd been overtaken, but I'd also been brazen enough to enter their building alone. Four of the most feared vampires had gone in together.

My heart raced as I paced the office. I was tempted to text someone, but couldn't risk distracting anyone from the mission. Finding Tap and Soleil—and even Carter—was the priority.

I hated doing nothing. It would have been a lot easier if Victoria were still awake. Then I could focus on her, but she only had the energy to stay awake a few minutes.

That made me feel like someone had ripped out my heart and stomped on it. Anger burned in my gut and surged through the rest of my body. I needed to do something, and yet I couldn't leave Victoria.

I pulled out my phone and texted Brick.

> **Toby:** How's it going?
>
> **Brick:** They r still inside.
>
> **Toby:** Have u heard anything?
>
> **Brick:** No. Some vamps r talking about going in.
>
> **Toby:** Where's Jet?
>
> **Brick:** With the queen.
>
> **Toby:** Should I be there?
>
> **Brick:** We got this. Stay with V.
>
> **Toby:** Let me know if anything changes.

It felt like I was going to explode. Despite Jet being a perfectly capable alpha, I was meant to be with my pack while they were out there, fighting for my fiancée. I couldn't be in two places at once, yet I needed to be.

I hated this.

I'd sent everyone else to the Jag, but now I needed to head over there—even if only for a few minutes. Was there anyone who could watch Victoria?

Alex. He was already pacing around the mansion.

No. It would never work. If something happened, he had no way of contacting me. He could hardly use a cell phone with paws. But he *could* fight off a perpetrator. He could howl into the sky. We'd all be able to hear him from the Jag given that it was only about two miles away if you went straight through the woods.

I turned around and glanced at Victoria. I'd never been more conflicted in my life.

"Are you awake, wolf?" I asked my inner wolf.

You think I could sleep at a time like this?

"What should we do?" I went over to Victoria and ran my palm across her cheek.

We won't be happy either way. If we join the wolves, we'll fret about her. Also, what if someone breaks in and snatches her?

I wanted to scream. He was right. There was no good answer. "What about Alex? Is it a bad idea to leave him with her?"

My wolf didn't answer. It was a risk, and we both knew it. Yet neither of us could deny the pull of the pack.

If anything happens to her, you know you'll blame yourself.

Again, he was right. On the other hand, if anything happened to anyone in the pack, I would never forgive myself, either. With great responsibility came high levels of guilt. Any blood would be on my hands, regardless of my decision.

She's sleeping, and from the looks of it, will remain that way for a while. Why not bring in Alex and set the house alarm?

The alarm. That was it—I'd receive a text the moment anything happened.

I kissed Victoria's forehead and then wrote her a quick note. Heart thundering, I went to the front door and whistled.

Alex trotted up to the porch. I indicated for him to come inside. He raised an ear, questioning.

"I need to check on the pack, and that means you need to keep an eye on Victoria. I'll leave a window open, so howl outside if anything goes wrong. She should just sleep—that curse is growing worse each day."

He whined, and I led him into my office.

"You don't have to relieve yourself, do you?"

Alex plunked his rear on the ground.

"I'll take that as a no. I'm also setting the alarm, so don't try to leave the house. Just howl. I won't be gone long."

He got up and went over to the couch, sitting in front of Victoria.

I took a deep breath. "If anyone shows up—"

Alex growled, baring his fangs.

"Looks like you know what to do. Thank you."

I went back over to Victoria, brushed some hair from her face, and kissed her lips lightly. "I'll be right back, my sweetness. All of this is for you."

She didn't even stir.

It killed me to leave her, but it had to be done. I needed to check on the pack.

I hurried out of the house, setting the alarm before I did. It took a couple tries because I wasn't used to setting it—there was always someone home.

If only I could howl into the sky to let the others knew I was on my way. Oh, well. They'd figure it out soon enough. I took a deep breath, stretched my legs, and then burst into a run, heading for the Jag.

I could feel the tension in the air long before I reached the jaguars' property. My heart raced faster than my legs.

Had something gone wrong?

I pulled out my phone and texted Brick, letting him know I was on my way.

He didn't respond. Come to think of it, he hadn't responded to the last text I'd sent him.

Something was definitely wrong.

My stomach twisted into a tight knot. Why hadn't I noticed earlier? I ran faster, darting around trees, branches, exposed roots, and shrubbery. My pulse drummed in my ears.

What I wouldn't give to be able to shift whenever I wanted. But that was a whole other curse, and I had no time to think about it. Finally, the strong jaguar scent came into the air. I was near the club. That meant my pack wasn't far away.

I sniffed the air, but when running it was harder to detect the direction of the scents. I just headed for the club. When I neared it, I slowed, both listening and sniffing the air. Both the jaguars and my pack were in the immediate area, as were the vampires, but for the moment I was including them with the pack.

My muscles ached, so I slowed further. Jet was close. I crept around a couple trees and found him crouched behind a bush.

He turned to me, eyes wide and fists clenched. Then relief swept over his face. "Toby, what are you doing here?"

"Where's Brick?"

"Around the other side of the building. He wanted to be closer since Soleil could be in there."

My mind spun. "Did he say anything about not answering his texts?"

Jet's brows came together. "Huh? What do you mean?"

"I mean he's not answering my texts." I glanced around,

but anyone in the area was staying well-hidden. "He answered a few earlier, but then stopped."

Jet swore. "Do you want to run around to the other side of the building to check on him? Everyone already knows I'm here."

"Yeah, that's fine. Where exactly is he?"

"Probably near where you were held. He just said he was going around to the back."

"Okay. I'll find him." If he was there.

Judging by the expression on Jet's face, he was thinking the same thing.

I burst into a run again. My muscles begged me to continue resting. I ignored them and pushed my limits. As I darted through the woods, I kept a lookout toward the Jag. Plenty of expensive cars sat in the parking lot, but I didn't see a single person outside the building. I passed several from our group, hiding and watching.

My heart thundered in my chest and my stomach continued tightening. Brick had spent years—centuries—with me. The thought of something happening to him made me sick. I slowed as I came around to the back of the building.

Sweat broke out along my hairline. I would never forget my time of torture in that building. I hated thinking that my friends could be in there, experiencing the same thing. Tap was tough, but small. The jaguars could easily gang up on him and cause real damage. I wasn't sure about Soleil—I'd have thought they would've been the ones in real danger—but who knew what kind of witchcraft they had access to. If they could remove Victoria's ability to shift, could they take away a valkyrie's ability to drink essence? I shuddered at the thought.

I slowed and sniffed the air again. This time, I caught a whiff of Brick. He was either a little ways off or he'd been where I was recently. I jogged, keeping my focus on the building. Everything appeared normal.

My right foot slid out from under me. I had stepped in something slippery, and despite windmilling my arms and trying to regain my balance, I fell to the ground. The ground felt spongy, and I was instantly covered in dark liquid that soaked into my clothes. I inhaled sharply and smelled blood. A lot of blood—it was Brick's. My own blood went cold.

What had gone down, and why had no one noticed?

I glanced around, trying to figure out where Brick had gone. The blood had to have dripped wherever he went—it was a significant loss, which meant a dangerous wound.

Fury burned in the pit of my stomach. I rose and glanced around, finally seeing the trail of blood. It led to the Jag, exactly where I had entered before being ambushed and captured.

My phone beeped. I didn't recognize the tone. Then I remembered.

The house alarm.

Alex howled in the distance.

CHAPTER 26

Toby

ALEX HOWLED IN THE DISTANCE again. My phone continued beeping. Someone was at the house, and only Alex—in wolf form—was there with my Victoria.

I jumped to my feet and ran. My feet slid, still wet with Brick's blood.

Sal appeared, his face pale. "What's going on, sir?"

There was no time to explain anything. I pointed to Brick's blood and headed back for the house, running faster than I'd ever gone before. If my muscles protested, I couldn't feel them. Sal and the others had to take care of Brick and our other missing friends. Victoria was my priority.

My heart felt like it was being shredded by vicious animals.

At last, Moonhaven came into view. The house alarm wailed and shrieked. I hadn't heard Alex since I was back behind the Jag.

My breathing constricted. I pushed myself to run faster until I reached the porch. The alarm wailed.

The door was broken down. Pieces lay scattered both in-side and out. Terror and anger gripped me. I slid my hand under the porch swing's cushion and grabbed a dagger I'd hidden away for a situation such as this. I gripped its wooden handle and crept inside. My senses were on fire, waiting to hear or smell anything and react at a moment's notice.

I crept inside and turned off the alarm. Then I headed for the office, but as soon as my shoe made contact with the hardwood floor, it suctioned to the bottom from the sticky blood. *Squelch, squelch, squelch.* I cringed and took off my shoes, throwing them outside. I walked quietly down the hall, hearing nothing. Not even the sounds of breathing.

Heart thundering, I headed for my office. Alex lay in the middle of the room, unmoving. A front leg stuck out at an unnatural angle and blood covered his mouth. I ran over and put my hand to his nose.

Faint puffs of air warmed my hand. I breathed a sigh of relief. At least he was alive and had likely done some damage to the intruder.

Victoria wasn't in the room. The blanket that had been covering her lay half on the floor and half on the couch. My heart dropped to the ground and my throat closed up.

"Victoria!"

My voice echoed around me.

I crouched down and sniffed the blood on Alex. It was werewolf, but I couldn't place the exact person—it was vaguely familiar. Maybe someone from Victoria's pack of origin.

"Victoria!" I shouted so loudly my throat hurt.

Alex lifted his head and opened one eye.

"I hope you're going to be okay, because I have to find Victoria."

He let out a small whine and lowered his head.

"I'll be back." I ran through the entire lower level, not finding any trace of her.

My phone vibrated. I had a text.

Sal: *Someone just ran into the Jag w/ Victoria.*

The room spun around me. It took three tries to reply to the text.

Toby: *Who? Was she OK?*
Sal: *Werewolf. That's all I no.*
Toby: *Someone has to go after her!!*
Sal: *Jags r everywhere.*
Toby: *Ill b right there.*

I ran to the broken front door. As stupid as it felt given the shape of the door, I set the alarm. At least it had motion detection to let me know if anyone came inside, since I couldn't keep anyone out.

My mind raced as I slid on a pair of shoes and then headed back to the Jag. I sniffed to determine whether I could smell Victoria or her captor. I couldn't. The breezy autumn air only gave me the aroma of leaves on the ground.

The jaguar stench grew thick. My inner wolf growled, scratching to get out. He was trying to force a shift—which was impossible. Obviously, that wasn't enough to stop him. Pains shot out through my entire body.

"I'd let out you if I could. You have to stop."

The muscles in my legs burned, cramping and throbbing. I was too close to the Jag to slow down and fight my inner wolf.

Finally, I made it to where Jet was hiding. I stopped, leaned against a tree, and panted. "What's... going... on... now?"

He arched a brow at me and ducked behind a bush and looked around. "They found some of the vampires—"

"And who... went in?" My lungs now burned along with my legs. I silently pleaded with my inner wolf to let it go.

"The king, his brother, and some other guy. Anyway, they all came out just before a bunch of the jags did. Now those cats are prowling the woods."

"In human form, or did they shift?"

"Both."

"Great. They haven't found anyone, have they?"

He shook his head. "Everyone is paired off, and nobody's texted me or yelled. If anyone hollers, we all jump into action."

I nodded, knowing the plan well. I'd taught it to him. "Where's your partner?"

Jet flicked his head toward the right. "Ziamara's hiding up in a tree."

My left leg cramped so bad I had to sit. I gritted my teeth and rubbed it. "Sal said... someone ran inside... with Victoria?"

He frowned. "I was hoping you hadn't heard."

"Why not?"

"It's harder to focus when the one you love is in danger."

"We need to get in there."

Jet turned around and waved someone over.

Ziamara jumped from a tree, landing without a sound and came over. She looked me over, her eyes wide. "What happened to you?"

"It's Brick's blood."

She flinched. "We've got to get inside. Now."

I nodded my agreement.

Jet slid his finger around his screen. "Okay, I just texted everyone. They're waiting for a signal to go."

I took a deep breath. "Then give it."

Jet nodded and then looked up to the sky. He shouted out a war cry that was unique to our pack.

Several others returned it. The sounds shot out from all directions in the woods.

From the corner of my eye, I could see several jaguars snap to attention in the parking lot.

My heart raced. This was it. Our chance to save Victoria and the others.

The jaguars released a war cry of their own—in unison.

CHAPTER 27

Victoria

SOMETHING PULLED ON MY ARM, waking me. My entire body hurt and my wolf whined. Or was that me? The tugging on my arm continued. I opened my eyes, expecting to see Toby or Alex.

Instead, Franklin's face appeared in front of me.

I bolted upright, despite my weakness. "What are you doing here?" I glanced around, realizing we weren't at Moonhaven. We were in what appeared to be a hotel room. I lay in a bed, covered. He sat next to me, on top of the covers. "Where did you take me?"

He rubbed my arm. "We're at the Jag, my fiancée."

"The Jag?" I skittered away from him, backing into the wall that the bed was against. "Why?"

"We need their magic to get rid of your spell." He scooted closer and rubbed his palm along my bare arm.

I glanced down. Someone had changed me out of my clothes. I was now wearing very revealing, blue lacy lingerie. Gasping, I pulled the covers up to my chin.

Franklin's dark, bushy brows came together and he pouted. "Oh, don't be like that, Tori."

"My name is Victoria."

"I've always liked Tori. You'd best get used to it."

My heart thundered in my chest. I glanced around for an escape. The room had no windows and the door had a latch on the top. It wasn't ideal, but it wasn't impossible, either. "When can I shift again?"

"After we marry." He pressed his wet, gross lips on mine, slurping and smacking.

I tried to turn away. My skin crawled. It took all my willpower not to shove him. I had to wait until I had an open escape.

He pulled back and smirked. "Don't forget—werewolf marriages are forever. Divorce and separation aren't words in our dictionary."

"Then how did you just say them?"

"Because the human world makes it necessary to bring them up."

I pulled the blankets closer and higher. My mind raced to find a way out. I'd rather die again than marry Franklin for even a moment.

He leaned against the pillows next to me, forcing the blankets out of my grasp. I grabbed them and covered my chest as best as I could.

Franklin crossed one leg over the other and sighed. "Do you know how long I've waited for this? To finally take hold of what's rightfully mine? I don't know anyone who's had to wait so long. But you're in luck, because I'm a patient man."

I clenched my jaw, refusing to entertain his sick and twisted thoughts.

He turned to me and stared at me with his muddy brown

eyes. "Do you remember our plans?"

My nostrils flared. Even though I refused to speak, I couldn't hide my disdain for him.

"You're going to give me one pup after another while keeping our large house immaculate. Nothing I love more than to come to a clean home at the end of the day, and even better with plenty of pups. Nothing shows the power and virility of a man like a litter of strong, healthy boys. That's why I can't wait to see you barefoot and pregnant year after year. You'll give them their good looks and they'll get their brains from me. Together, we'll make the perfect werewolves."

It took all my energy to keep my mouth from dropping open. I wouldn't have thought it possible, but he'd actually grown even more obnoxious and full of himself over the years.

The corners of his mouth curved up. "I've left you speechless."

At least he finally spoke the truth.

Franklin ran his fingers along my shoulder and down my arm, before sliding his fingers through mine. He shivered. "You're even more delectable than I imagined."

My stomach lurched at the thought of *what* he had imagined.

He yanked the blanket away from my grasp and ogled me. "And you look just as I pictured when I picked that out."

I yanked my hand free of his and crossed my arms over my chest.

"You're no fun." He leaned over and kissed me with his wet, disgusting lips again. "But you're right. This really should wait until after the wedding. I'm acting inappropriately." He backed up and climbed off the bed.

I grabbed the covers and held them up again. Exhaustion hit me once more, leaving me no other choice than to lie down. I struggled for my breaths.

"Tiring out already?" He arched a brow. "We'd better get our wedding going so we can rid you of that spell." He reached up to the top of the door and unlocked the latch.

My heart raced. If he opened the door, I would have my chance to escape. Except that I didn't have the energy to crawl across the bed. I wasn't even sure I could roll over.

Franklin started to open the door, but then stopped. He kept his focus on me and strutted back to the bed. "One thing does disappoint me, Tori."

I sighed, not even having the energy to protest the nickname.

Slowly, he strutted across the room with his hands on his waist.

Sleepiness overtook me, making it hard to keep my eyelids open.

"Look at me when I'm speaking."

Inside, I cringed. Or was that my wolf? I forced my eyelids open and glanced at him.

"The spell makes you weaker when you think poorly of me. I was hoping you'd be stronger, but that can't be blamed. Tobias has you wrapped around his pinky, and somehow the two of you have found each other and teamed up again. That ends now. You'd best rid your mind of that loser."

I opened my mouth to defend Toby, but a fresh wave of exhaustion engulfed me.

"See what I mean about the curse?"

"If that's true…" I gasped for air. "How did I manage to…

fight you off before?"

"Clearly, you didn't think too badly of me then."

Or because I hadn't thought of him *at all* until he showed up in Seattle, chasing me.

The door burst open.

"Victoria!"

Carter!

CHAPTER 28

Toby

A GROUP OF TEN JAGUARS ran toward us, one after another shifting into their animal form. I reached for the dagger and held it close. Jet and I would stand a better chance if we could shift, but that wasn't a possibility. We would have to make do in our human form.

The one in the lead lunged for Jet. He jumped out of the way, and Ziamara jumped on top of him, her eyes red. She opened her mouth, exposing sharp fangs and bit into the jaguar's neck. He let out a yelp and flung himself onto the ground, rolling on top of her. Jet jumped on the jaguar. I raised my weapon, but had to focus on the other nine enemies heading our way.

Ziamara rose and flung the animal to the side. "I've got enough venom to take out a couple more."

Jet turned toward the other nine. "Then the others are on Toby and me."

I clenched the blade's handle. Jet and Ziamara ran toward the oncoming group. I sniffed the air. Other werewolves weren't far away.

Two jags avoided them and headed straight for me. I

leaned against the tree, needing to rely on its strength. The first beast raised his front legs into the air, seemingly in slow motion, right for me. As he came down, I dug the dagger into his throat. He gurgled, choking. Blood dripped down my arm and he fell to the ground, whining.

Before I could even take a breath, the other lunged at me. I moved out of the way, and he crashed into the tree's trunk. I sliced in to his chest and spun around just in time to see another one headed right for me.

His teeth dug into my shoulder before I could respond with the dagger. Pain seared as my flesh tore, probably as deep as the muscle. I sucked in a deep breath and dug the blade into his side. He yelped and let go of me. I shoved him away and dug the blade near his neck.

Whining, he dragged himself away from me.

"You think you're getting away that easily?" I jumped on top of him, slicing through his fur and into his skin until his eyes closed and his head rested on the dirt.

Marguerite ran over, her eyes wide. "Toby!"

A jaguar jumped at her from behind.

"Look out!"

She spun around and in one quick motion, bit into his neck. His eyes rolled back and then his head fell forward. Then she turned back to me. "I wish they were all that easy. Most of the jaguars are harder to kill than other species I've fought—and I've fought a lot of nasties."

"Please just find Victoria."

"No, *you* find her." Marguerite pulled her sleeve up and bit into her wrist. "Drink."

The mixed blessing of having a royal vampire in battle

with you. Her blood could heal me, but I had to drink it in order for it to work.

She shoved her wrist to my mouth, giving me no choice. The metallic smell tickled my nose.

Dillon appeared from behind a tree. "Wait! Won't that kill him?"

"Only my venom has that capability," Marguerite corrected. "Vampire blood will heal him. Mine will give him more energy than he had before getting hurt." She turned back to me. "I said drink."

My stomach turned at the smell, but I had no other choice. I put my lips to her wound and sucked. The cool, bitter blood filled my mouth.

Dillon's face contorted as he watched. "I hope I don't need that," he muttered.

Jet shoved him. "Just kill some more jags. Now."

"My pleasure." Dillon ran toward the parking lot.

"Focus on me." Marguerite guided my face so that I was looking at her. "We're going to beat these shifters, and you're going to save Victoria. You're already her hero—I can see it in her eyes."

Strength formed within my core. I wasn't sure if it was from the pep talk or the blood. Probably both.

"You can do this, Toby. You've helped win wars. I know it's harder to focus when someone you love so dearly is at stake, but you have to focus."

"You're right." I focused on drinking. When the energy circulated, coursing its way through my entire body, I let go and steadied myself.

"Did you get enough?" she asked.

"I think so. Let it run through my system. You need your strength, too."

She shook her head. "I'm more worried about you. I can drink from Alre if I need to."

The energy buzzing around my insides flashed with an inexplicable burst. I jumped to my feet and glanced around. All of my senses seemed on fire. I could see farther, hear more acutely, and smell more scents. My muscles no longer hurt, but begged to be used.

We ran around to the back, taking down jaguars as we went. It didn't take long to gather a good-sized group. We would definitely give them a run for their money, if not take them down completely. It just depended on how many they had in there.

"Do you see an opening?" Sal asked, as we wandered back around to the front.

The front door burst open.

Carter ran outside.

"I thought he'd been taken captive," Jet grumbled.

"That's what I thought," I said. Had he actually been in on it, breaking Victoria's trust?

Carter waved us over. "Hurry!"

"So we can fall into your trap?" Jet yelled.

"No! It's Victoria! Get in here!"

My heart plummeted to the ground.

CHAPTER 29

Victoria

FRANKLIN TIGHTENED HIS GRIP AROUND my wrists. I cried out in pain.

He turned to me and slapped me across the face with the back of his hand. "I've had enough of you."

"Then why marry me?"

"Because you're mine. Now shut up." He yanked me down the dimly lit hall. The little lights along the path reminded me of all the happy times I'd been there with Carter. Between this and having rescued Toby, the Jag was nothing more than a horrible memory—all good ones there had practically been erased.

My right foot twisted and I stumbled over the too-long slacks he'd made me wear before leaving the room and sending Carter away.

Franklin turned around and glared at me. "Have you always been this pathetic?"

I clenched my jaw, keeping myself from spitting in his face like I wanted to.

"Well, I'll just have to beat the clumsiness and stupidity out of you. Hurry." He pulled me forward again, dragging me behind him. "Now keep up."

Footsteps sounded down the hallway. It sounded like a herd—or a pack. Toby?

I whipped my head around.

"Don't get too excited," Franklin said. "Those are probably just our wedding guests."

My stomach lurched. If only I had something in my stomach to throw up—all over him. "What did you do to Carter?"

"Why do you care?"

"Because he's my friend."

Franklin spun around and glared at me. "Sure he's nothing more?" He sprayed hot spit on my face.

"My heart only belongs to Toby."

He scowled. "You need to let him go. Look at all the heartache your rebellious fancy for him has caused. You should have seen your poor mother after you and Elsie died. It nearly killed her as well."

I flinched, hating to think of what Mother had gone through—all at the hands of her husband. He'd killed Elsie personally, and though he hadn't pulled the trigger, he was behind my death, too. If he'd have let me marry whoever I chose, I'd have never died in the first place.

The footsteps behind us grew closer. I sniffed the air. Vampires and werewolves.

My heart thundered in my chest. Had the pack come for me? Did Franklin know they were coming?

Franklin's grip around my wrists tightened all the more. He would leave bruises for sure.

I needed to find a way to stop the wedding. There was no way I would agree to marry him, but he would find a way to force me. He would soon find out how serious I was about choosing death over a life with him.

He stopped in front of a closed door. "Here we are. I think seeing this room will change your tune."

I said nothing. The only thing that would change my mood would be if Toby was in there with open arms, waiting for me—which of course was a joke. If Franklin had his way, the next time we stepped into this hall, we would be married.

What a scumbag.

My eyes grew heavy and the exhaustion engulfed me like a thick fog. He had to be speaking the truth about my irritation toward him making me weak.

I fell to the ground. The only thing keeping me from collapsing all the way was his death grip on my wrists. He shoved me up and against the wall. "Quit it."

The footsteps down the hall finally caught up to us. They belonged to my father, brothers, and several of his key wolves. My heart sank. I would have sworn I'd smelled vampires and wolves from our pack.

Had that only been a trick?

My father sneered at me. "Looks like you're finally where you belong. It took you long enough. You'll learn to obey our ways soon enough."

I stared at him. He hadn't changed a bit—he was the same man who had killed his daughter so many years ago. Without a doubt, he still fully believed he had done the right thing in murdering Elsie. What an outdated relic he was, and a colossal sexist besides. I couldn't keep my feelings and a sneer from showing on my face.

Franklin shoved me into the wall. "Show your father some

respect. I won't have my wife behaving like this."

Good thing I wasn't his wife.

He shoved me again, this time digging his nails into my flesh. "Did I not make myself clear?"

Several of the men laughed.

"Can't control your woman, huh Franklin?" asked Henry, one of my father's closest advisers.

The whole group roared with laughter.

Franklin's face turned red—I could see that much in the dim hallway. He forced me against the wall, knocking the back of my head against it. "Pay respects to your father, woman."

Tears stung my eyes. I turned to my father and held his gaze. "Yes, sir." I couldn't remember what he'd said, but that seemed like a reasonable response—or at least something they would find acceptable.

Father folded his arms and looked down on me. "Glad to hear it. Let's get this wedding over with. You owe Franklin a huge apology for making him wait so long. Centuries! I've never met a man so patient. He knew you'd come back to him one day."

I didn't respond.

"I said you owe him your sorrow, daughter."

Franklin's grip tightened even more.

Shaking, I turned to him. "I-I'm sorry."

"For what?" He pulled me close, so that I was pressed against him. I could feel the rhythmic motion of his chest as he breathed.

"For making you wait so many years."

"Don't worry. You'll make it up to me." He opened the door and forced me into the small room. A couple dozen chairs pointed toward the front of the room, otherwise there was no other indication that a wedding was about to take place. My stomach twisted into a tight knot, but somehow I felt more energized.

Because I'd apologized to Franklin.

What if that was it? If that was my out? Perhaps if I faked going along with the wedding, I could build up enough strength to get away. It would be tricky with the strongest and most agile men of our pack in the room, but it was my only chance.

"Get to the front." Someone shoved me from behind.

Franklin dragged me to the front. Everyone else shuffled into the seats.

My heart threatened to explode out of my chest as I tried to think of a way out. "Don't I need a dress?"

"Stupid human tradition," Franklin muttered. "Doesn't matter what you wear."

"Can you let go of my wrists?"

"I *can*, but I won't."

"I won't go anywhere."

He snorted, clearly seeing through me. "I don't trust you, even with your father and the rest of his men here. You're going to have to earn my trust after everything you've pulled."

"But you said I need you to be able to shift, right?"

"Yes."

"Then why would I flee? The last full moon nearly killed me. One more without you, and it certainly will."

"Stop talking."

"But I—"

"I said, stop talking."

It looked like I would need to take a different angle to make my escape. I glanced around the room. Seeing my father and his chauvinistic crew made my skin crawl.

The door opened. My head snapped to attention. Could it be Toby?

My mother and some of the other women from the pack entered. Elsie wasn't with them. Did that mean she had managed to hide from the pack, also? Or had they hurt her again?

Mother covered her mouth when she saw me. She and the others sat next to their husbands like the obedient wives they were—just as I would be expected to behave if I couldn't find a way out of the ceremony.

Something crashed into the other side of the wall. My breath caught. Was *that* Toby or our pack?

"Don't look so excited." Franklin jerked my arms. "It's just the jaguars. They like to wrestle."

I believed him about as much as he believed I wouldn't try to make a run for it if given the chance. I sniffed the air, trying to see if I could still smell my real pack. Unfortunately, I couldn't smell any over the pack in the room.

The door opened again.

My pulse raced.

A man with thinning gray hair and a wrinkled suit came inside. "It's crazy out there!"

"You're here now," my father said. "Let's get this show on the road. We have a great many wrongs to right that this will fix."

The room seemed to shrink, closing in on me.

"Of course. Glad to see you got her in time."

My father nodded. "They sure didn't make it easy, but ultimately, we always get what we want. One way or another." He turned to me and stared at me. I couldn't pull away from his gaze.

The door opened again.

"What?" Franklin muttered. "Everyone's here."

Toby walked in and glanced around. His gaze stopped on me.

CHAPTER 30

Toby

EVERYONE ELSE IN THE SMALL room turned and glared at me. Memories raced as I scanned the room. So many people I'd killed before the other side released the dead. Eyes narrowed, faces reddened, and growls sounded around the room.

Clearly, many wished to repay me.

Finally, my gaze landed on the front of the room. Victoria stood at the front, wearing a pale yellow top that buttoned up to her neck and black pants that covered her shoes—clothes that women used to wear in the packs years ago. Franklin had a hold on her, and she had to be in pain, given the angle he held her wrists.

Anger tore at me. "What's going on?"

Her father rose, taking off a large hat. "You need to leave. Your kind isn't welcome here."

"That should be up to Victoria."

He glowered at me. "It's up to her father as head of the pack and her husband."

I felt like I'd been punched in the gut.

This was a wedding.

I turned to Victoria. "You've *married* him?"

She shook her head vigorously. "No, I—"

Franklin pressed her against the wall. She cried out.

I ran down the aisle, but all the other men in the room jumped up to block me.

"You were told to leave," said one of Victoria's brothers.

"Not without her."

"Don't do this. Let her have her wedding."

"Look at how he's treating her!" I tried to get around them, but they had me blocked on all sides.

"Exactly as she deserves." Her father scowled. "After what she put everyone through. In fact, I'd think you'd find her too much trouble after nearly getting you killed."

I pushed against them, but as a group, they were too strong.

"Stop," her father told the others.

They all let go, and I lost my balance, nearly stumbling, but I recovered quickly and glared at him. There was no way he'd tell his guys to back off unless he had something worse in store.

The look in his eyes made my blood run cold. "What is it?"

He threw back his head and laughed a cruel, dark laugh. "The only way Victoria will be able to shift again is if she marries Franklin. Then as part of the family, he finally becomes my second-hand man."

I stared at him, too dumbfounded to speak. Could it be true?

"In other words," Franklin said, "get out!"

The men around me roared with laughter.

My pack and the vampires were waiting outside in the hallway. It was tempting to release my war cry and have them all pile in, but if Victoria needed to marry Franklin in order to shift, I couldn't risk him getting killed.

Not yet, anyway.

"How do I know you're telling the truth?" I demanded once the laughter quieted. "What does him marrying her have anything to do with her shifting?"

Franklin narrowed his eyes. "Because it's the only way to cure her of the curse keeping her from shifting. The jaguars asked what I thought a good cure would be, and that seemed fitting. Now step aside."

My stomach sank. It fit everything else we knew—everything Victoria remembered from the *true love's kiss* spell. She recalled the jaguars setting everything up with her father and mine to mess with her mind. One of the witches had stripped her ability to shift, and her father knew she would need to undo that, so he made sure it would end up in the marriage he had always wanted so badly.

I would have to kill Franklin in between saying the *I do*'s and the consummation of the marriage. Then I would take great joy in killing everyone behind the cruel curse. How dare they put Victoria through such agony after everything she has already been through?

"I *said* to move."

I glanced around the room, trying to decide how to handle the situation. It was risky, but I had to let her marry the pompous wolf. At least long enough to break her free. Then death could part them. My gaze finally landed on her. She pleaded with her eyes for me to do something. Unfortunately, that meant continuing with the ceremony. I gave her a quick nod to let her know I had a plan.

I turned to her father. "Carry on with the ceremony. If you're going to keep me from her, I want to see this with my own eyes."

Victoria cried out.

He laughed. "Even better." He turned to his sons. "Keep hold of him."

Victoria's three brothers came over to me. Two of them grabbed onto my arms and dragged me to a seat. The other sat, glaring at me.

I looked up at Victoria, giving her an expression that I hoped showed her I had a plan.

The pain in her eyes told me the message wasn't received.

"Are we ready?" asked the officiant.

The look on Victoria's face nearly killed me. She may as well have cut out my heart with a dull knife, chewed it up, and spit it back out at my feet.

She had to know the last thing I would ever let happen would be for her to *actually* marry that moron. But if it was the only way for her to shift, a temporary wedding had to happen.

I couldn't let her die. Not again.

CHAPTER 31

Victoria

TEARS STUNG MY EYES AS I stared at Toby. Not only was he covered in blood—whose?—but he just sat there, letting my good-for-nothing brothers hold him down while I was about to be forced into marrying Franklin.

I took a deep breath and studied his face. He didn't seem worried. Maybe that meant he had a plan. Could he have found Soleil? If so, was she out in the hall, waiting to suck out the essence of every other werewolf the room besides Toby and me?

That had to be it. He wouldn't give up that easily.

Franklin squeezed me, digging his nails into my skin again. "Look at me, woman. You've seen the last of that fool."

"Don't you want her to watch us kill him?" my father shouted.

I flinched.

"Of course she will," Franklin sneered, glaring at me. His grip tightened all the more.

I gasped and pulled away. He dug his nails, drawing blood, and pulled me so close I was pressed against him.

"You don't want to see that?" he taunted.

The officiant moved, blocking my view of Toby. Unfortunately, that was probably for the best since I needed to think about Franklin in order to build my stamina. Maybe I could try to kill him once we became man and wife. The thought of being married to him for even a minute made my stomach lurch.

"We are gathered here," the officiant began.

Franklin loosened his grip around my wrists slightly. "Look at me."

I turned to him and forced myself to look into his eyes. It was almost impossible to not hate him, but I had to find something redeemable about him. Exhaustion was already forming in my joints.

Holding his gaze, I thought back to my days growing up. Once, when we were kids, Franklin had fought off a bully for me at school. Granted, it was because he already thought of me as his property, but still, he'd protected me from a werewolf nearly twice my size.

The fatigue lifted, but I didn't feel especially strong. I needed to focus on more good he'd done. Every time I thought something bad about him, I felt worse.

Finding anything positive about the self-deluded weasel would be a challenge.

He'd never spent any time trying to get to know me. Not like Toby had. He treated me like a prized gift—each new thing he learned about me was a treasure he held dear.

Franklin had always kept his distance, only coming near to remind me of my future role as his maid and baby-making factory.

My muscles ached.

I wasn't helping my situation any.

The officiant rambled on about the importance of marriage in the werewolf community when preserving the truest form of tradition—which basically meant the worship of the alpha and other male leaders.

My knees gave out, and I stumbled. Franklin yanked me up.

A scuffle sounded in the audience.

"Sit back down," one of my brother's barked.

The long rambling about the institution of marriage continued.

I sighed and continued trying to think of something—anything—good about Franklin. If that was what would save me, I was clearly in trouble.

Something crashed on the other side of the wall, out in the hallway. My pulse drummed in my ears.

"Hurry up." Franklin glared at the officiant. "Just get to the end."

"These things can't be rushed."

Franklin let go of me and grabbed the officiant's collar. "Yes, it can."

This was my chance.

I stepped back and looked for something I could kill Franklin with while everyone was distracted.

Horrible pain shot through my muscles. Fatigue washed over me like a rushing waterfall.

I fell to the ground, unable to move.

Shouts and screaming echoed around the room. Toby's war cry sounded above the rest.

The door burst open and banged against the wall.

"Kill Toby!" my father shouted.

CHAPTER 32

Toby

I JUMPED AWAY FROM THE wolves holding me down—they were shocked and distracted by the commotion. My pack and the vampires filed into the room.

Everyone jumped into action. Victoria's former pack all surrounded me. My pack closed in on them. I took advantage of the mass confusion and leaped over the chairs in front of me, heading for Victoria.

She lay on the floor, unmoving. Franklin had his fingers wrapped around the officiant's neck. I darted around people and pulled Victoria into my arms.

"Franklin," she whispered.

"No, it's Toby. I'm going to get you out of here."

"Have… to… marry—"

"I know, but we'll find a workaround. I swear."

She shook her head. "It won't work."

"But Gessilyn—"

"Already tried."

"Franklin!" someone shouted.

Hands grabbed my shoulders, ripping me away from Victoria. I reached for her, but she was too far now. Franklin pulled on my shirt, choking me. "You aren't going to ruin this wedding! It's bad enough that you made her miss the first one."

"She was *dead*," I grunted and pushed his arms, forcing him to release his hold on me. "And you'd better believe I'm going to stop this wedding, too." I spun around and wrapped my fingers around his neck. What I needed was to reach my dagger.

Someone grabbed me and dragged me away. I looked back to see Victoria's father.

"Finish the ceremony!"

Franklin ran over to Victoria and scooped her up. "We're ready."

The officiant looked at him like he was crazy. "With everyone fighting?"

"Hurry!"

I struggled against Victoria's father. His grip was stronger than I'd have expected. But it was no match for a blade. Gagging, I reached for my dagger. I had to wiggle it out from my pocket carefully due to the angle. Finally, it came loose.

His focus was on the front of the room.

The officiant shouted, "I now pronounce you man and wife!"

Anger surged through me. Over my dead body would the farce of a marriage go further. It wasn't real unless Victoria agreed—and from where I stood, she was unconscious.

Her father let go of me to clap and shout. I spun around and dug the knife into his gut. His eyes widened, and he covered his wound as redness spread across his shirt.

I turned to the front of the room.

Franklin pressed his slimy lips onto Victoria's.

"No!" I cried and ran to him, gripping the blade as tightly as my fingers would allow. I pushed aside the officiant and lunged for Franklin.

He glared at me and let go of Victoria. She fell to the ground, landing with a harsh thud.

"You know, someone who loved her wouldn't do that." I held the blade behind my back.

Franklin sneered. "I never claimed to love her. Doesn't make her any less mine—especially now that she's my wife."

I glanced over at her. "The marriage doesn't seem to be helping her any. I thought it was supposed to help her shift."

"Idiot." He rolled his eyes. "It has to be consummated—have fun imagining that. I've spent enough time thinking about it."

I punched him across the face. My fist seemed to act on its own.

He shook his head. "She also won't be able to shift until the full moon. Know any werewolves who can shift whenever they want?"

"You're unbelievable."

"No, you are. Thinking you have any right to her without her father's permission." His fist hit my cheek with a loud crack. He hit me with his other one before I could react.

Blood gushed from my nose and my cheek felt hot as it swelled. I was done playing.

I brought the dagger out and forced it into his throat, digging it as far as it would go before pulling it out.

His eyes widened and blood gushed from the wound. He opened his mouth, but no words came.

"That's right. I win."

A blinding light filled the room. I covered my eyes and squinted, trying to figure out where it was coming from. It seemed to be close, like it was right next to Victoria.

No, it was coming *from* her.

CHAPTER 33

Victoria

ENERGY RAN THROUGHOUT MY BODY. A powerful warmth radiated everywhere, starting from my mole.

My inner wolf jumped around excitedly inside. It took me a moment to realize I could get up. I rose, feeling stronger than I had in a long time. I looked around the room—it was chaos. Toby stood not far away, holding a bloody knife. Blood covered his clothes.

Our gazes locked and then he jumped over the body at his feet and wrapped his arms around me. "I think we broke your curse."

"But I didn't marry Franklin." I paused. "Or did I? I'm so sorry, Toby. I tried to stop him."

"He's dead. It doesn't matter anymore."

A sharp pain ran through my back. I cried out.

His eyes widened. "Are you okay?"

The pain ran down my arms and legs. I stepped away from him. "I'm going to shift. I need to get out of here."

"Wait—now?" He stared at me, his eyes even wider.

"Yes." I pulled away from his embrace and ran from the room, darting around people fighting.

"Stop!"

I was pretty sure that was Toby, but I couldn't wait. I darted down the dark hallway. Pains ran through my neck and down every bone in my body. I had to get somewhere private to throw off my clothes.

A rib cracked, and then another. Hopefully, I could get out of the building first. The process was happening a lot faster than it ever had before. Cracking and popping sounded all over my body. The pains made it hard to run. I stumbled.

Arms reached around me. "I'm here," Toby said. "You're shifting now?"

I nodded, not trusting my voice.

"Okay, I'll get you outside in time. Then run as far from here as possible. Go to either Moonhaven or the Faeble."

"I will."

Fur sliced through my skin. I cried out in agony.

Toby turned down a hallway and we came to a door. He opened it, and bright sunshine shone in. We ran out into it.

He let me down and stared into my eyes. "I love you."

"Me, too." I ran behind a pile of wood leaning against the building and threw off my clothes as my bones continued breaking and fur cut through my skin.

In a flash, the world changed around me. No, I had finally shifted into my wolf form. Everything looked different from wolf's eyes during the day. I looked up into the sky, seeing no moon, and howled.

Footsteps and scuffling sounded from near where Toby was.

"Run," he cried.

My feet seemed to act on their own. I darted away, going

around the backside of the building, just as he'd told me. But then I skidded to a stop. I couldn't just leave. Not when he and the pack were fighting my old pack and probably the jaguars, too.

I ran back to where Toby was and slowed, hiding behind the wood again. He and my brothers were fighting. I growled and then jumped out from my hiding spot, heading for my youngest brother. His fist was about to hit the back of Toby's head.

My legs seemed to move on their own as I lunged for him. My paws made contact first, and then my teeth sank into his shoulder. He cried out, shrieking in pain as I tore into his skin. His blood soaked into my white fur.

"Stop her!" My oldest brother jumped for me. Toby blocked him and dug his knife into his chest. Blood sprayed everywhere.

My middle brother lunged toward them. I dropped my youngest brother. He fell to the ground, moaning. A deep growl escaped from my throat as I aimed for my last remaining brother.

His face paled, and the smell of his fear surrounded me.

Toby dug the blade into his throat and shoved him to the ground. "I won't let any of you pompous bullies hurt Victoria." He turned to me. "I thought you were going to run. We've got this. I don't want anything happening to you. We'll find Tap and Soleil—I promise. Maybe you should check on Alex."

My ears rose. Alex? What was wrong with him? I whined.

"He got hurt trying to stop Franklin from taking you."

My paws nearly slid out from under me on the hot concrete as I broke into a run, heading for Moonhaven. I hoped Toby was right about finding the others because I needed to check on our wolfborn. He was every bit as much a part of the pack as anyone else, and if he was hurt, I had to see what I could do.

As I ran through the woods, I finally felt in my element. Everything rushed by in a blur as I moved with grace, darting over and around things. Could my clumsiness finally be gone?

The smell of ash tickled my nose. A crackling noise sounded. I slid to a stop and sniffed the air. Creeping quietly, I followed the stench out of the woods. In the distance, flames danced around the Jag. Thick, black smoke rose into the air, darkening the sky. Cries and screams sounded from the building.

My heart raced. Should I check on Alex or head back to the Jag to help everyone else?

Toby *had* told me to go to Moonhaven. He was the pack's alpha, and as a wolf, it was in my nature to follow his directions. However, things had changed. The Jag was on fire. Everyone could be in danger. Alex might be, as well. If he'd been hurt since Franklin took me, he might need my help more than the others.

I glanced back and forth between the Jag and the woods, never more conflicted. But the worst thing I could do was nothing. I burst into a run, heading for Moonhaven. Alex was alone. He needed me more than the others. And at least I could communicate with him since both of us were in our wolf forms.

My muscles burned—in the best way possible—as I tore through the woods, kicking up dust and dirt along the way. It felt so good to be in my wolf form again, running like I was meant to.

Finally, the mansion came into sight. I picked up speed. My heart raced, nervous for what I would find. What if Franklin had killed him?

I skidded to a stop when I reached the porch. The front door was missing.

What happened? Trepidation ran through me. I hurried up to the door and ran inside. At least that made it easier to get in. I sniffed the air and whined, calling for Alex.

Scratching sounded from Toby's office. Hadn't that been where I had rested last? It was hard to remember—everything from when I had been sick and weak felt like such a distant memory, almost like it had happened to someone other than me.

I ran into the office. Alex lay on the floor. He lifted his head and stared at me.

It's just me—Victoria.

His ears perked up. *What? How?*

It's a long story. Where are you hurt?

Everywhere. He lay his head back down.

Anger burned through me. *Franklin did this?*

A werewolf did. I don't know his name.

I leaned down and took a closer look. He appeared to have blood around his face and neck. *What did he do?*

He kicked me and threw me across the room when I tried to stop him from taking you.

Do you have any serious injuries?

Bruising and a broken leg. It should heal when I shift.

I growled. *At least he's dead now.*

The guy who did this?

Yeah, Toby killed him. Then I shifted.

Are you like a wolfborn now? Spending most of the month as a wolf?

I froze. That couldn't be, could it? The last thing I wanted was to shift on the opposite schedule as Toby. I sat down and howled, overcome with grief.

It actually isn't that bad. There are more like us—we just have to find them.

I'm not a wolfborn. I think I only shifted because my curse broke. In fact, I might shift back at any moment. I hoped.

Do you smell smoke?

The Jag is on fire. With any luck, the jaguars will all leave the area.

You think they will?

I don't know. Can I help you with anything?

Actually, I'm thirsty.

What was I supposed to do about that as a wolf? I couldn't walk into the kitchen and pour him a glass of water.

Brick keeps a bowl for me outside, around back.

I can't bring it in. Not like this.

Drag me. I've got three good legs.

It was worth a try. I went over and gingerly bit his scruff and pulled. He rose, with his legs shaking. I moved around to his other side, seeing which leg was hurt. Together, we managed to get him outside and around to the bowl of water. He collapsed and emptied it.

I wandered along the yard, staring at the blackening sky.

Where was everyone? Why weren't they making their way back yet?

Alex turned to me. *What now?*

I was hoping you could tell me. I howled as loud as my voice would allow, pausing only to take a breath. Then I howled again and again, determined not to stop until the pack came back home—hopefully with Carter, Soleil, and Tap.

Fear and worry ran through me. What if something happened after I left? Had the jaguars attacked the pack while they were exhausted from saving me?

A sharp pain ran down my back from the base of my skull to the end of my tail.

So soon? I whined, anticipating another painful shift.

Alex glanced over at me. *Are you okay?*

I think I'm going to shift again.

Sharp pains ran down all four legs and radiated up and into my ribcage. I bolted toward the front of the house and ran inside, up to my room. I struggled up the stairs as the bones in my legs cracked along the way.

Once inside the bedroom, I lay on the floor, giving into the shift. The fur retracted and each bone in my body snapped, one by one. Finally, the entire process ended. I was human again.

Footsteps and voices sounded outside. The pack was home. Hopefully everyone had made it through unscathed.

I scrambled to my feet and pulled clothes from my closet.

CHAPTER 34

Victoria

I RAN DOWN THE STAIRS. Some aches lingered, but otherwise I felt energized—which was probably a good thing. Many in the pack probably needed help after all the fighting.

Conversation drifted from downstairs and outside. I tried to weed out the individual voices, eager to find out who had survived. I hadn't seen anyone from our pack get hurt, but with all the fighting back at the Jag, it seemed unlikely that we would come out completely unscathed.

As I reached the bottom of the stairs, everyone was coming inside.

I ran over and wrapped my arms around Toby.

His face lit up and he pressed his lips on mine. "You shift-ed back. How do you feel?"

"Like I could take on the world."

Toby glanced around. "Where's Alex?"

"Outside, by the drinking bowl."

He glanced at Brick, who had fully healed from his jaguar attack. "Bring him inside."

Brick spun around and hurried outside.

Toby turned back to me. "When did you shift back? How

long did it last? Was the process—?"

"Slow down." I held back a laugh. "It was a pretty normal shift. Well, minus the moon. I'd never changed during the day before, so that was strange."

He held me tight. "I'm just trying to figure out what all this means. Can you turn any time you want? Or was this a one-time deal because of the curse finally breaking?"

"I have no idea, but I wasn't trying to shift when I did."

"We'll just have to wait and see, then. I'm so happy your curse is broken. You feel good now?"

"Like I said, I feel great."

"This is so amazing. I can hardly believe it."

"What happened back at the Jag? I could see the flames."

His expression darkened. "We took out most of your old pack, but a half-dozen or so were left. One of them set fire to the Jag, but it backfired because he caught the attention of the remaining jags, and they took off after him. The others scattered. From the sounds of it, the remaining jags went after them."

My stomach twisted in knots. "What about Tap and Soleil? Did they get out?"

Toby's expression worsened.

I felt like I was going to be sick. "What? What happened?"

"Dillon went to find them, but…" He looked away.

"What?" I exclaimed.

"He found Tap being held where I was before, and he freed him. But one of the jaguars killed Dillon."

"Dillon's dead?"

Toby nodded, his eyes filling with anger.

"Where's Tap? Soleil?"

"Tap got away while Dillon was fighting. He was in bad shape—nearly as bad as the jags left me. He said he had medicines at the Faeble he could take, so I sent one of the vampires to take him there. I'm sure Quinn is helping him as we speak."

"You don't know where Soleil is?" I exclaimed. Fear tore through me. "And what about Carter? I saw him before the wedding, but not after."

"Nobody could find her. She had to have teleported herself away. It's the only explanation."

"While they were beating Tap up?" I shook my head. "I don't buy it." Hot, angry tears blurred my vision. "We have to do something."

"She'll come back when she feels safe. Brick and Tap are also both anxious to find her."

My stomach twisted in tight knots. The room seemed to spin around me. "Carter? Do you know anything about him?"

"I didn't see him after he came outside and told us you were in there."

Stars danced before my eyes and I gasped for air. It was all too much.

Sharp pains ran through my body. Some popped. A few crunched.

I was going to shift again.

"Victoria?" Toby stared at me, wide-eyed.

The pains ran in waves up and down my body. I needed to get out of the house. Immediately.

I broke free of his hold and ran outside. Fur began to slice through my skin. I ran to the back of Moonhaven, hoping no one from the pack was there. I stripped, having no time to look around, much less worry about modesty.

The rest of my fur sprang out, cutting my skin, and my bones all broke one by one as they changed shape.

For a second time that day, I was in my wolf form. I looked up at the sun, barely visible from the smoke in the air, and howled before running into the woods. I needed to find Soleil and Carter. Everything went by in a blur as my legs rushed me through the thick forest.

When the Jag came into view, the flames were gone. Thick black smoke rose from the ground, where the building used to be. The entire thing had burned to the ground. I sniffed the air, trying to determine how many jaguars remained. It was hard to tell with the recent fire. The only thing I could smell was the soot and smoldering ash.

Only a few cars remained in the usually full parking lot. Many had likely fled.

Sirens sounded in the distance. I needed to check the grounds for my friends before the firefighters, police, and other emergency vehicles arrived. Even though the narrow road leading to the Jag would have made it difficult for the large vehicles, they would arrive soon.

I ran toward the smoking rubble that had been such an elegant club. If anyone *was* inside, I couldn't see how they would have survived. As pointless as it probably was, I continued sniffing the air.

The sirens grew louder.

I howled and then hurried into what remained of the club. I ran through the familiar floor plan, finding no one. It seemed that everyone had cleared the building. I stopped at the top of the stairs leading down to their holding cells. Half the stairs

at the side of the house. If anyone was inside, I would annoy them until they came out.

After a few minutes and the start of a sore throat, I could hear the sounds of a window opening.

"Quiet!"

My heart skipped a beat. It was Carter. He was okay.

I whined, hoping he would figure out that it was me.

"Go away!"

That hadn't worked. I howled again, throwing my head back and forcing my voice as loud as it would go.

He slammed the window shut.

I rushed over to the front door and scratched on it, continuing to whine and howl.

After a couple minutes, the door flung open. He stared at me, his expression exasperated. "I said to go away! What's so hard to understand about that?"

Why couldn't I get him to understand he was looking at me? I pressed myself against his legs and nudged my nose against his palm.

"What the…?" He stared at me. "Victoria?"

I whined.

"You shifted? Now?" He stepped back and turned into a black and yellow jaguar before my eyes, his clothes shredding in the process. *What's going on? Why are you here?*

I had to find out if you were okay.

Yes, but I have to get out of here. Most of the jaguars are fleeing back to Central America.

You're not, are you?

I can't. They see me as a traitor.

My chest constricted. *What are you going to do, then?*

I have to start over somewhere. I'm packing what I can. Dad has cameras in there—that's how he knew I was working with you guys.

Join our pack.

His eyes widened. *In case you didn't notice, I'm not a wolf.*

We have a vampire in our pack. There is also a family of witches who practically live there with us. I'm sure no one will notice a jaguar.

Right.

I'm serious. Come with me. We have to find Soleil, anyway.

She's on her way to the Faeble.

I stared at him. *How do you know?*

She called me, looking for you. Said she'd heard Tap needed help.

My mind raced. *You're sure it was her?*

She said she had to make like a banana and split.

Relief washed through me. *That's her. Do you know why your father took her and Tap?*

They were too close to the truth. Father wanted them both killed, but they both fought too hard. They sent some of our strongest jaguars to the infirmary.

I was impressed. *I'm going to the Faeble to check on Tap. Maybe he knows where Soleil is. Promise me you'll at least stop by Moonhaven, okay?*

Why? So you can try to talk me into joining the pack?

Maybe, I teased, only half-kidding.

Let me at least drive you.

To the Faeble? In the middle of the woods?

I can get you close.

I shook my head. *I'm fast in this form. I'll meet you at Moonhaven in an hour.*

Okay, but I can't promise I'll stay.

Just be there.

I promise. Oh, and don't take this as a pickup line, but you're the prettiest wolf I've ever seen.

Don't say stuff like that in front of the pack.

Trust me, I'm not stupid. See you in an hour.

Be there. I turned around and ran off, giving him the privacy to shift back into human form.

I headed for Moonhaven, which was about halfway in between Carter's place and the Faeble. An ache ran through my bones. I was going to shift back already?

Groaning, I picked up my speed. The pains intensified, but I forced myself to go faster. It was apparent that I would need to place spare clothes in key locations.

Finally, the mansion came into view. Bones in my tail popped. I hoped I had enough time to get to where I'd left my outfit behind the building. I ran over and crashed to the ground. My body shifted and I gasped for air before scrambling for my clothes. I slid them on and hurried inside.

Conversation drifted from the kitchen—not that it was any big surprise. Everyone was probably famished, and there was no better place for tired wolves to unwind than over a meal.

Toby stood at the stove, stirring something in a large pot. Everyone was there, except Brick and Dillon. My heart constricted as I stared at Dillon's empty seat. In fact, the mood in the room was somber and the conversation mellow.

I went over to Toby and wrapped my arms around his waist. He turned and looked me, relief covering his face. "What happened? Why did you shift again?"

"I don't know. It just happened, but I did find out that Soleil is at the Faeble."

He kissed me. "I know. She called shortly after you left. Brick tore out of here to see her."

"Carter's okay, too." I paused, careful with my wording. "He's without a pack, though."

Several around the table turned and stared at me, obviously aware of what I was suggesting.

"Are we going to bring in a jaguar?" Sal asked.

Toby turned to Jet. "What do you think?"

"You're asking me now? I can't stop beating myself up for being so hard on Dillon. I was a jerk, and now he's dead."

Ziamara put an arm around his shoulders. "He's not dead because you were a jerk. It's not your fault."

"No, but it may as well be."

I frowned. "Jet, nobody blames you."

"Except me."

"It's a tough lesson to learn," Toby said.

Jet rose and pushed in his chair. "I need some time alone."

"We need to talk about Carter," I said. "We can't make a decision without you."

He hung his head. "I'm in no position to make a decision about anything. You guys do what you think is best." He sulked out of the room. Ziamara jumped up and ran after him.

I made eye contact with everyone at the table. "Carter has nowhere else to go. He's already lost his place in his pack because he sided with us. We should let him in."

"What do you think, Toby?" asked Sal.

Everyone looked at Toby.

CHAPTER 35

Toby

THE FLAMES ROARED TO LIFE, dancing around the fire pit. In the background, the full moon was just starting to appear in the horizon.

"Who wants marshmallows?" Brick opened a giant bag.

"Don't forget the chocolate." Soleil grinned as she opened the box of candy bars.

"Let me help with those." Carter pulled out a handful of them. "Wait. You guys are canine. Should you have any?"

"Just don't feed any to Alex." Jet glanced down at our friend, sleeping at his feet in wolf form.

Victoria turned to me and smiled. "This is fun, and best of all, we're together."

I wrapped an arm around her and kissed her cheek. "Are you sure you're going to be able to shift? Your body has to be exhausted with as many times as you've changed since the curse broke."

"Maybe the full moon will set me on course, and I'll only shift when everyone else does."

"Either that, or you're going to have to get control over your emotions."

"Hey!"

"You can't deny that every time you shift, it's when you're upset or excited about something."

She shrugged. "Maybe. I'm just glad everything is settling into a new normal again."

"And I'm glad my wolf and I aren't at constant odds anymore. It'll be nice to shift and simply be as one. All the back and forth bantering wears us both out."

Victoria laughed. "I can imagine. I'm grateful that my shifts have been seamless."

Brick handed us marshmallows. "Better get to roasting. The moon will be in place soon."

I shivered. "And it's cold enough to snow."

"That suits me." Victoria snuggled against me.

We all laughed and joked as the moon moved higher and higher into the sky. The younger wolves got up and started pacing first.

"What are you guys doing?" Soleil exclaimed. "We still have about twenty bars of chocolate."

"We don't exactly have much of a choice here," Slick grumbled. He rubbed his neck. "In fact, I need to bolt." He ran into the thick of the woods, pulling his shirt off along the way.

I turned to Victoria, moved my hands over the back of her neck, and sprinkled kisses on her soft, sweet mouth. "It's going to be so nice to run with you again. Even better without worry of running into our old packs."

She gazed into my eyes, frowned, and rested her hand on my chest. "I can't feel the shift gearing up. Not even in the slightest."

I leaned over and whispered in her ear. "You'll shift. *I* can feel it. We're going to run together tonight." I skimmed kisses from her ear to her mouth.

"I hope you're right." She didn't look convinced.

The rest of the wolves got up from their spots and headed into the trees.

Aches ran down my spine. "I am, but first I need to shift. I'm coming right back here and waiting for your shift so we can run free."

Victoria nodded. I squeezed her hand and then hurried out of sight before I found myself shifting in front of her, Soleil, and Ziamara. I didn't care if Carter saw me. He was a shifter, and used to the lifestyle.

My bones felt like they would explode as I threw off my clothes. Fur cut through my skin and in a matter of moments, I was in my other form. I couldn't hear the voice of my wolf—that meant we were finally one again. It felt like it had been a lifetime.

I ran back to the bonfire. Victoria still sat with the others. Alex was in his human form, roasting a marshmallow. I went over and nudged her with my nose.

She rubbed my scruff and looked at me with tear-filled eyes. "I'm so sorry, Toby. I know how badly you wanted this."

I put my paw on her lap.

Tears spilled onto her face. "I've let you down."

You haven't! She couldn't hear me.

Victoria put her hands over her face and sobbed. "We're never going to be wolves at the same—ow!" She jumped up and ran into the thick of the trees.

Alex glanced over at me. "It's all going to work out. Soon, we'll all be able to change when we want. Just like the jaguars."

I hoped he was right.

"If I can find out how we were able to break the moon's curse, I will," Carter promised.

Victoria, in her gorgeous white coat, ran over. *Luckily, I freaked out since that's what seems to make me shift.*

I shouldn't have put so much pressure on you, but I'm glad you shifted. Ready for a run?

Like you wouldn't believe. She nudged me and then ran off.

I chased after her, catching up.

With Victoria at my side, the moon above, and the rest of the pack howling, everything finally felt right.

What will happen next? Will Victoria and Toby ever find the cure to the curse of the moon, and be able to shift whenever they want?

Find out more in Hunted Wolf,
coming soon!

Learn more and see the gorgeous first four covers here!
stacyclaflin.com/books/curse-of-the-moon

Other Books

If you liked Chosen Wolf, you might enjoy the Transformed series where it all began...

The Transformed Main Series

The Gone Saga

The Seaside Hunters series

Visit StacyClaflin.com for details.

Sign up for new release updates and receive three free books.
stacyclaflin.com/newsletter

Want to hang out and talk about books? Join My Book Hangout and participate in the discussions. There are also exclusive giveaways, sneak peeks and more. Sometimes the members offer opinions on book covers too. You never know what you'll find.

facebook.com/groups/stacyclaflinbooks

Sneak Peeks

Sweet Desire is the story of Gessilyn discovering that she's the high witch...

Fate can only be avoided for so long. Gessilyn's time is up.

She has been living a quiet life, pretending to be human for many years, but now she's a witch on the run. Her old coven has found her—and they want Gessilyn dead.

If she's to survive, Gessilyn must return to her roots and learn magic from a father she never knew. The power within her reveals itself to be stronger than she can handle. As a result, Gessilyn finds herself more of a risk to herself than anyone else is until she can learn to control it.

While needing to focus on all she has to learn, Gessilyn finds herself increasingly drawn to Killian, the handsome loner in her father's coven. She tries to ignore her growing feelings, but they only intensify. Will she be able to hone her powers in time to defeat her old coven, or will Killian distract her and be her downfall?

Preview:

The moon's glow on my skin tingled. Then it intensified to a near-burn. It shone full and bright. I gritted my teeth and ignored the discomfort. My pain indicated something more ominous coming.

Cawing from a murder of crows disrupted the quiet of the

night. I shuddered at the irony of the group's name because they announced ominous things to come. They circled the outline of the moon. It gave them an eerie glow. They grew louder.

"Is this a warning for me?"

Silence.

Several woodland creatures scurried away.

Goosebumps formed on my arms and neck. I swept my long hair to the side and twisted it around my manicured nails. The moonlight made it seem especially blonde.

I took a deep breath and ran a finger along the skirt of my dress. "Do you have a message for me?"

The black scavengers flew erratically, completely blocking my view of the moon. Their cawing sounded more like screams. I wanted to cover my ears but refused myself the comfort. The noise became deafening.

I squatted to the ground, refusing to leave. I needed to figure out their message.

The birds dispersed and disappeared from sight as quickly as they'd appeared.

Gasping for breath, I stood and steadied my shaking arms. My heart thundered in my chest. I was no closer to understanding the message, but I had ways of finding out.

Saved by a Vampire is the story of Ziamara and Jet:

Vampires. Witches. Werewolves. Betrayal.

Ziamara nearly died, but a distantly-related vampire put a stop to that. After training to live safely among humans, she returns to her hometown of Delphic Cove to settle into her afterlife. Things are as normal as can be, until a pack of werewolves try to tear her limb from limb.

She survives the assault but returns home to find her house destroyed. Her grandmother is missing, and the only ones who can help her are the very werewolves who threatened her afterlife! Neither Ziamara nor the wolves are excited to work together, but one member of the pack has caught her eye. At a time when the new vampire needs to focus, the only thing she can think about is him.

When Ziamara and the pack get closer to the truth about her grandmother's disappearance, they find something more ancient, powerful, and deadly than they ever imagined...

Preview:

My mouth watered at the rare smell of bacon and eggs. My favorite. We seldom found scarce commodities like pigs and could barely afford bacon or other cuts if we did.

"Come down for breakfast, Ziamara," called my grandma.

"Hold on!"

The food smelled heavenly, although what I really wanted was something else entirely. Delicious, red liquid. But I only had one bag remaining, and I couldn't waste it. Not when I wasn't sure where the next one would come from.

Staring at my reflection, I found it hard to believe I'd recently faced death's door. Though a bit paler than it once was, my complexion had never been better. Not a single mark marred my skin—no reminders of my long hospital stay.

I rose and went over to my full-length mirror, turning from side to side. My bones no longer stuck out from all my lost weight. In their place were some lush curves, exactly where I'd always wanted them. I smiled, never having been so pleased with how I looked.

Regardless, I threw on an old hoodie. I would draw enough attention, and I didn't need my figure to add to that. Another day.

I ran a brush through my newly long, thick shiny brown hair. Even prior to being sick, it had never been so full of life.

How ironic, considering I was now technically dead.

Okay, I'd been more than just at death's door. I'd passed through, coming back on the other side. It's all semantics.

Author's Note

Thanks so much for reading Chosen Wolf. I hope you enjoyed it as much as—or more!—than Lost Wolf. I'm really enjoying the series myself, having always been a fan of Toby's since the *Transformed* series. I'm glad that he is finally able to find love!

Feel free to let me know your thoughts. I'd love to hear from you. The easiest way to do that is to join my mailing list (link below) and reply to any of the emails.

Anyway, if you enjoyed this book, please consider leaving a review wherever you purchased it. Not only will your review help me to better understand what you like—so I can give you more of it!—but it will also help other readers find my work. Reviews can be short—just share your honest thoughts. That's it.

Want to know when I have a new release? Sign up here (stacyclaflin.com/newsletter) for new release updates. You'll also get a free book!

I've spent many hours writing, re-writing, and editing this work. I even put together a team who helped with the editing process. As it is impossible to find every single error, if you find any, please contact me through my website and let me know. Then I can fix them for future editions.

Thank you for your support! I really appreciate it—and you guys!

56197662R00164

Made in the USA
Columbia, SC
21 April 2019